CHRONICLE
IN STONE

CHRONICLE IN STONE

A NOVEL

ISMAIL KADARE

Arcade Publishing
New York

Arcade Publishing books may be purchased in bulk at special discounts
for sales promotion, corporate gifts, fund-raising, or educational purposes.
Special editions can also be created to specifications. For details, contact the
Special Sales Department, Arcade Publishing, 307 West 36th Street, 11th
Floor, New York, NY 10018 or info@skyhorsepublishing.com.

Arcade Publishing® is a registered trademark of Skyhorse Publishing, Inc.®,
a Delaware corporation.

Visit our website at www.arcadepub.com.

10 9 8 7 6 5 4 3

Library of Congress Cataloging-in-Publication Data

Kadare, Ismail.
  [Kronikë në gur. English]
  Chronicle in stone : a novel / Ismail Kadare ; translate from the Albanian by
Arshi Pipa ; edited with an introduction by David Bellos.
    p. cm.
  Originally published in Albanian as Kronikë në gur.
  ISBN 978-1-61145-039-2 (pbk. : alk. paper)
  1. World War, 1939-1945--Albania--Fiction. I. Pipa, Arshi, 1920-1997. II.
Bellos, David. III. Title.
  PG9621.K3K713 2011
  891'.9913--dc22

                               2011001767

Printed in the United States of America

INTRODUCTION

Ismail Kadare was born in 1936 in Gjirokastër, an ancient, stone-built city in southern Albania clinging to the steep sides of a hill topped by a huge fortress, part of which has been used for centuries as a prison. Close to the Greek border, Gjirokastër was badly mauled by several armies during the Second World War. In April 1939, Mussolini occupied Albania and annexed it to the short-lived Italian Empire. In 1940, the Italian Army stationed in Albania invaded Greece, but was repulsed and routed by the Greek Army supported by the RAF, which carried out heavy bombing raids over many parts of Albania between 28 October 1940 and 30 April 1941. In a counter-attack, the Italians retook the southern part of Albania: Gjirokastër then changed hands several times over. When Italy capitulated to the Allies in September 1943, the German Army, which had meanwhile invaded and occupied Yugoslavia and Greece, took over the whole of Albania, and occupied strategic points like Gjirokastër.

Chronicle in Stone narrates these traumatic events in the life of the city through the eyes of a dreamy, short-sighted, and highly imaginative child, whose thoughts and interests (in girls, murders, hermaphrodites and homosexuals) seem to make him a little older than Kadare actually was at the time. But the chronicle stops short of the war's real ending. The German Army collapsed and withdrew from the Balkans in the summer and autumn of 1944. With Yugoslavia, Albania was the only country in Europe to be liberated without the help of significant Allied forces. The Communist partisans, led by Enver Hoxha, entered Tirana in November 1944, and established a People's Republic, which turned into Europe's most long-lived, most bizarre and probably cruellest Stalinist regime. It crumbled only after the fall of Gorbachev and the failure of the Soviet "generals' putsch" in August 1991. The omission from this memoir of a war-time childhood of the conventional narrative of national liberation by Communist partisans must be counted as a sly but perfectly visible act of literary resistance.

There were three separate national resistance movements in wartime Albania. The least significant was *Legaliteti*, a movement formed by supporters of the exiled King Zog (who ruled from 1924 until 1939), and which operated primarily in the northern parts of Albania. It barely figures in Kadare's narrative, save as a rowdy gang referred to as "Isa Toska's men." The second main non-Communist group was called *Balli Kombëtar* ("National Front"), whose members were called *Ballists*. They figure more substantially in *Chronicle in Stone*, both as the perpetrators and as the victims of irrational violence. The third and by far the most effective resistance group were the partisans, organised and quickly dominated by the Albanian Communist Party. Isa and Javer, the two young men admired by the child narrator of this book, are members of this movement and share its political aspirations. Although Kadare does not deal with the liberation itself in this novel, his picture of a city divided between Ballists, Partisans and "Isa Toska's men" carries the clear implication that the struggle for freedom was something close to a civil war. Once again, this was significantly different from the official version of the birth of the socialist state.

Chronicle in Stone was not written all at once. It first emerged as an anecdote about "The Big Plane," which was among Kadare's earliest publications in prose, appearing in the literary review Nëntori in 1962. (The child's fascination with aircraft is strangely similar to J. G. Ballard's account of his own early years in Japanese captivity in Empire of the Sun.) Together with more anecdotes about his childhood and his early misapprehensions of the world and of words, Kadare reworked "The Big Plane" into a longer story of Gjirokastër, "City of the South," which similarly appeared in a periodical in 1967. It was not until 1971 that an expanded, reworked and re-ordered novel entitled Chronicle in Stone appeared as a book. But that was only the beginning — for Kadare is an obsessive rewriter of himself. Chronicle in Stone went through several editions in Albania, each incorporating larger or smaller developments, until it was finally brought into Kadare's multi-volume Complete Works series, published by Fayard in Paris in 1997, in strictly parallel French and Albanian versions. For this definitive text, Kadare made many changes. Some dialogue passages were tightened up, others expanded; some historical and political passages were cut, and other passages — whole pages of conversation between some of the stranger old ladies of the town, for example — were added. But even this definitive version may not be quite the end of the story. In 2004, while spending a month as Writer in Residence at Bard College, New York, Kadare wrote an entirely new short story, "A Climate of Lunacy," set in Gjirokastër during the author's childhood, and introducing more of the curious and entertaining characters in the family circle that we meet in *Chronicle in Stone*, written forty years before.

Like most of Kadare's fiction, *Chronicle in Stone*, was translated into French before appearing in other languages. For hazy editorial reasons that seem to have been lost, the French translation by Jusuf Vrioni was entitled *Chronique de la ville de pierre*, (Chronicle of the City of Stone), and it is by that title that the book is still widely remembered in France. However, its real title is simply *Chronicle in Stone* (*Kronikë në gur* in Albanian), and in Kadare's *Complete Works* in French it has been retitled to conform, as *Chronique de pierre*. Like the monument built by Cheops in Kadare's later parable, *The Pyramid*, the real message or mystery of Gjirokastër is not *written on stone*: it *is* stone.

One of the central characters in the life of Kadare's child-narrator is his maternal grandfather. In Albanian, the mother's father ("the line of milk") is named and treated somewhat differently from the father's father ("the line of blood"). The familiar term used by the child, *babazoti*, literally means "father-lord," the second half of the word also serving to refer to God (just like "the Lord" in English). In this translation, I have for the most part translated *babazoti* by "grandfather" or "grandpa," but left the original term here and there so as to communicate the flavour of a now vanished form of family life.

Babazoti lies on a divan all day reading books in Turkish, for he is old enough (in 1941–3) to have spent his youth and manhood as a citizen and official of the Ottoman Empire, which only relinquished its control of Albania in 1913. The old women who particularly fascinate the child are all the daughters, widows or wives of Albanian Muslim landowners, or of officials of the former empire, and it is to the Ottoman past that they owe the relative prosperity that allowed them to construct the large and mysterious houses that provide the child with such a rich source of imaginative life. Among them is a group of centenarian women, the "old crones," and a fearsome group of somewhat less aged old ladies known as "the mothers-in-law," called *katenxhikas* in the dialect of Gjirokastër. Ottoman influence is also responsible for the *hashure* (a kind of halva) and hot *saleep* (orchid-root tea) hawked on the streets and even in the citadel when it is used as an air-raid shelter.

For the society depicted in this novel, the words "Greek," "Christian" and "peasant" are virtually interchangeable. Only a few words of Greek are known to the child, and this despite the fact that Greece itself is only a few miles from Gjirokastër. When the young revolutionaries Isa and Javer speak in a "foreign tongue" so as not to be understood by the little ones, the language they use is the Latin they learned in school. This is never stated explicitly in the novel because for Albanian readers of Kadare's generation it goes without saying.

Kadare was a city boy, with no experience of the land, and, as will be seen, without any inclination to discover the countryside at all. In the People's Republic, and in its official literature imitated from Soviet models, the life of agricultural workers was a conventional object of praise. The refusal of the little boys in this novel to entertain even the idea that "peasants' work" might be purposeful or comprehensible or anything other than a sham may strike us now as comical, but in Hoxha's Albania it must have felt like a daring provocation.

One of the most important events in the life of the narrator as told in *Chronicle in Stone* is the encounter with Shakespeare's *Macbeth*. The underlying material of that play — not just ghosts, witches and murder, but the dynamics of the struggle for power, the ineradicable nature of a crime committed, and the inexcusable flouting of the rules of hospitality — run through Kadare's entire work. In *The Concert*, one of Kadare's masterpieces, there is even a full proposal for a new version of *Macbeth*, the better to account for the death of Lin Biao, Mao Tse-Tung's designated successor. Kadare's explorations of the ancient Albanian rule of the blood-feud in novels like *Broken April* are also implicit meditations on Macbeth's true crime, the breaking of the *besa*, which grants guests protection from harm.

Chronicle in Stone is full of other plot-lines and story-fragments that will grow into a whole range of works set in varied times and locations. The legend of Ali Pasha of Tepelena, a local potentate (in whose court Lord Byron stayed for a time) whose severed head was exhibited in Istanbul, is recounted indirectly in *Chronicle in Stone*, but forms the explicit subject of Kadare's later novella, *The Nook of Shame*. The brief mention of the prostitute killed by Ramiz Kurti sends the reader back to *The General of the Dead Army*, where a fuller account of this honour killing is given. In other places we come across the fear of blindness, suggesting the matter of a later story, *The Blinding Order*; a book of dream interpretation, hinting at the magnificent fantasy of *The Palace of Dreams*; and pyramids of skulls — be they ascribed to Genghis Khan or to Timur the Lame — recur in stories as varied as *The Pyramid* (set in Ancient Egypt) and *The Great Wall*, set in China of the late medieval period. Even the outline of the bridge that requires a sacrifice to stay above the water — the subject of *The Three-Arched Bridge* — can be found in an aside in the thoughts of one of the characters in *Chronicle in Stone*. Not quite all of Kadare's work is inscribed in the stone city of Gjirokastër, but the strong images of his childhood — *Macbeth*, slaughter, severed heads, propitiatory sacrifice, the instability of words and sounds, and the battle of wind and rain — are the stuff out of which much of his later works are made.

Chronicle in Stone was translated into English by Arshi Pipa, an Albanian intellectual who was imprisoned in the early years of the Hoxha regime. He escaped, fled to Yugoslavia, then to Italy, and finally to the United States. A distinguished scholar of medieval Italian literature, Pipa was for many years Professor of Romance Languages at the University of Minnesota, but he also remained passionately committed to the fate of his homeland, and wrote many articles and books about Albanian literature in the Communist era. Initially, he was an ardent supporter of Kadare, in whom he saw not only a remarkable writer, but a cunning critic of the Hoxha regime. He undertook the translation of *Chronicle in Stone* in order to make Kadare better known in the West. Pipa's English was naturally Americanised, given his long residence in the USA, but he found a publisher for his work in the UK. The publisher's editor made numerous changes to Pipa's text, not only in order to impose British conventions on the text, but also to improve its fluency. Unfortunately Pipa took exception to the editing done to his work, and an increasingly acrimonious correspondence ended with the translator disowning his own work and requesting that his name be removed from the published book.

Pipa was also very angry that his own long introduction to the book was cancelled. Later published in an American journal, Pipa's essay is both hugely informative and more than slightly paranoid. The Gjirokastër that Kadare recalls, Pipa notes, is a city peopled by a curiously large number of sexual deviants, including a "woman with a beard" (which he takes to mean a lesbian), a homosexual husband and a hermaphrodite, and it is also a city in which many crimes are committed in connection with sex — a girl probably drowned in a well for kissing a boy she was not engaged to; a half-man, half-woman murdered in his bed for daring to get married; a prostitute murdered by the father of one of her clients for bringing dishonour on the family. Gjirokastër is also, famously, the home town of Enver Hoxha, the country's dictator, and this is made quite explicit in the text. Pipa argues that the depiction of the city is intended "by distant reflection" to raise the question of Hoxha's sexuality. Like most members of the Albanian elite, Pipa and Kadare both knew that in his youth (and in particular during his many years as a student in France) Hoxha had had homosexual encounters, but this was not something that could be written or spoken aloud in Communist Albania. Kadare was horrified when he heard that Pipa planned to assert that *Chronicle in Stone* contained a coded message about the sexual preference of the country's Guide. He honestly thought that Pipa wanted to get him arrested and shot. A long drawn-out polemic ensued, with attack bringing counter-attack, until the whole murky business became known as the "Pipi–Kaka Affair." It is no longer remotely dangerous to mention the probable sexual proclivities of a long-dead Stalinist — but it also now seems crazy to believe that this fine and complex novel contains any coded message on that subject.

Pipa's translation is the basic text of this edition of *Chronicle in Stone*. To Pipa's work I have added the passages included by Kadare in Volume V of his *Complete Works* in French, and deleted the passages that Kadare dropped. I have nonetheless retained the Albanian forms of the names of people and places (in the French edition, names are spelled in French transliteration) and I have not adopted the transpositions made by the French text of some of the historical and political references (turning "Ballists" into *collabos*, for example). I have also made stylistic amendments here and there where they seemed called for. For the most part, however, this English version of *Chronicle in Stone* is Arshi Pipa's, and to him the main credit is due.

Gjirokastër really is quite as spectacular as the description of it given in this novel. It has been in decline as an administrative and commercial centre throughout the twentieth century, and many of its large stone houses have been uninhabited for decades. In 1967, all religion was abolished in Albania, and most of the country's churches, monasteries and mosques were destroyed or put to other uses. At the same time, the regime sought to create and fortify the "national spirit," and to celebrate the country's more or less ancient traditions. Despite Hoxha's ambivalent feelings about the Ottoman heritage of his home town, he saved the city's mosque, and also had Gjirokastër officially designated as a "Museum City." It became an important centre of folk culture in socialist Albania, and was chosen to host the National Folk Festival, which was held there every five years. In 2005, after several failed bids, Gjirokastër finally became a UNESCO World Heritage Site.

The old Hoxha family house was converted into a Hoxha Museum in the 1970s. It was blown up by protesters in 1997. The family home of Ismail Kadare described in this novel has also been destroyed, by an accidental fire that swept through the neighbourhood in 1999. Plans are in hand for a faithful reconstruction of it.

The great citadel remains unchanged and its eerie vaults now house a museum of military hardware. On the open-air esplanade of the fortress described in this book stands the decaying fuselage of a US spy plane that had the misfortune to wander into Albanian airspace more than thirty years ago.

David Bellos
Princeton, N.J.
December 2, 2006

A NOTE ON PRONUNCIATION

Most letters of the Albanian alphabet are pronounced roughly as in English. The main exceptions are as follows:

c	*ts* as in *curtsy*
ç	*ch* as in *church*
gj	*gy* as in *hogyard*
j	*y* as in *year*
q	*ky* as in *stockyard* or the *t* in *mature*
x	*dz* as in *adze*
xh	*j* as in *joke*
zh	*s* as in *measure*

CHRONICLE
IN STONE

It was a strange city, and seemed to have been cast up in the valley one winter's night like some prehistoric creature that was now clawing its way up the mountainside. Everything in the city was old and made of stone, from the streets and fountains to the roofs of the sprawling age-old houses covered with grey slates like gigantic scales. It was hard to believe that, under this powerful carapace, the tender flesh of life survived and reproduced.

The traveller seeing it for the first time was tempted to compare it to something, but soon found that impossible, for the city rejected all comparisons. In fact, it looked like nothing else. It could no more support comparison than it would allow rain, hail, rainbows, or multicoloured foreign flags to remain for long on its rooftops, for they were as fleeting and unreal as the city was lasting and anchored in solid matter.

It was a slanted city, set at a sharper angle than perhaps any other city on earth, and it defied the laws of architecture and city planning. The top of one house might graze the foundation of another, and it was surely the only place in the world where if you slipped and fell in the street, you might well land on the roof of a house — a peculiarity known most intimately to drunks.

Yes, a very strange city indeed. In some places you could

walk down the street, stretch out your arm, and hang your hat on a minaret. Many things in it were simply bizarre, and others seemed to belong in a dream.

While preserving human life rather awkwardly by means of its tentacles and its stony shell, the city also gave its inhabitants a good deal of trouble, along with scrapes and bruises. That was only natural, for it was a stone city and its touch was rough and cold.

No, it was not easy to be a child in that city.

I

Outside, the winter night had wrapped the city in water, fog and wind. Buried under my blankets, I listened to the muffled, monotonous sound of rain falling on the roof of our house.

I pictured the countless drops rolling down the sloping roof, hurtling to earth to turn to mist that would rise again in the high, white sky. Little did they know that a clever trap, a tin gutter, awaited them on the eaves. Just as they were about to make the leap from roof to ground, they suddenly found themselves caught in the narrow pipe with thousands of companions, asking "Where are we going, where are they taking us?" Then, before they could recover from that mad race, they plummeted into a deep prison, the great cistern of our house.

Here ended the raindrops' life of joy and freedom. In the dark, soundless tank, they would recall with dreary sorrow the great spaces of sky they would never see again, the cities they'd seen from on high, and the lightning-ripped horizons. The only slice of the heavens they would see henceforth would be no bigger than the palm of my hand, on the occasions when I used a pocket mirror to send a fleeting memory of the endless sky to flicker on the surface of our reservoir.

The raindrops spent tedious days and months below, until my mother, bucket in hand, would draw them out, disoriented and dazed from the darkness, to wash our clothes, the stairs, the floor.

But for the moment they knew nothing of their fate. They ran happily and noisily across the slates, and I felt sorry for them as I listened to their wild chattering.

When it rained three or four days in a row, my father would push the gutter-pipe aside to keep the cistern from overflowing. It was a very large cistern, extending under most of our house, and if it ever overflowed, it could flood the cellar and wreck the foundation. As our city was all askew, anything could happen then.

As I lay wondering whether people or water suffered more in captivity, I heard footsteps and then the voice of my grandmother in the next room.

"Hurry, get up. You forgot to shift the down pipe."

My father and mother leapt from their bed in alarm. Papa, in his long white drawers, ran down the dark hallway, opened the little window, and pushed the pipe aside with a long stick. Now we could hear the water splattering into the yard.

Mamma lit the kerosene lamp and led Papa and Grandmother downstairs. I went to the window and tried to see out. The wind was furious, dashing the rain against the windowpanes, making the eaves groan.

I was too curious to stay in bed, and I ran downstairs to see what was happening. All three grown-ups looked worried. They did not even notice I was there. They had taken the cover off the cistern and were trying to see how high the water had risen. Mamma was holding the lamp while Papa leaned over the side and peered in.

I shivered all over and caught hold of Grandmother's dress. She put her hand on my head affectionately. The wind shook the doors inside and out.

"What a downpour," Grandmother said.

Papa, bent over, was still trying to see inside the cistern.

"Get a newspaper," he told my mother.

She did. He crumpled it up, lit it, and dropped it into the cistern.

"The water's almost up to the rim," Papa said.

Grandmother started murmuring prayers.

"Quick," my father cried, "the lantern."

Mamma, pale as wax, her hands trembling, lit the lamp. Papa threw a black raincoat over his head, took the lamp, and headed for the door. Mamma tossed an old dress over her head and went after him.

"Where did they go, Grandmother?" I asked, frightened.

"Don't be scared," she replied. "Neighbours will come to help with bailing out, and then the cistern will calm down . . ." Her voice became rhythmical, as if she was whispering an old tale: "In this world, each ill has its cure. Only death, my dear boy, has no remedy."

Muffled knocks at a door sounded through the rumbling of rain. Then again, and again.

"How can we lower the water, Grandmother?"

"With buckets, dear boy."

I went to the opening and looked down. Darkness. Darkness and a feeling of terror.

"A-oo," I said softly. But the cistern didn't answer. It was

5

the first time it had refused to answer me. I liked the cistern a lot and often leaned over its rim and had long talks with it. It had always been quick to answer me in its deep, cavernous voice.

"A-oo," I said again, but still it was silent. I thought it must have been very angry.

I thought about how the countless raindrops were gathering their rage down below, the old ones that had been languishing there so long getting together with the newcomers, the drops unleashed by tonight's storm, plotting something evil. Too bad Papa had forgotten to move the pipe. The waters of the storm never should have been let into our well-behaved cistern to stir up rebellion.

There was a noise at the door. Xhexho, Mane Voco and Nazo came in, with Nazo's daughter-in-law in tow. Then Papa came in, and Mamma, shivering with cold. The door creaked open again. This time it was Javer and Maksut, Nazo's son, carrying a big bucket.

I was glad to see so many people. Chains and buckets jingled. All the clattering seemed to lift the anguish from my heart.

I stood back a little and watched them all noisily setting to work: Mane Voco, tall, thin and grey; Nazo's son and her daughter-in-law, so pretty with her gentle, sleepy look; and Xhexho, breathing heavily. Mane Voco, Xhexho and Nazo drew buckets of water, which the others emptied into the yard. It was still pouring rain, and from time to time Xhexho would mutter in her nasal voice, "Good God, what a flood!"

As each bucket was emptied out, I said silently to the water, "Go on, get the hell out, if you don't want to stay in our cistern." Each bucket was filled with captive raindrops, and I thought it would be good if we could weed out the nastiest ones first, the ringleaders; that way we could lessen the danger.

Xhexho put down her bucket and lit a cigarette. "Did you hear what happened to Çeço Kaili's daughter?" she said to Grandmother. "She grew a beard."

"You're joking!" Grandmother said.

"May I be struck blind," said Xhexho. "A black beard, really, just like a man's. That's why her father won't let her out any more."

That got my attention. I knew the girl, and it was true that I hadn't seen her in town for quite a while.

"Oh, Selfixhe," Xhexho moaned. "What a life we lead! One bad omen after another the good Lord sends us. Like this flood tonight."

Xhexho, her eyes following Nazo's beautiful daughter-in-law, barely three weeks married, whispered something in my grandmother's ear. Grandmother bit her lip. I moved closer to hear, but Xhexho flicked her cigarette butt away and went to the edge of the cistern.

"What time can it be?" asked Mane Voco.

"Past midnight," my father said.

"I'll make you some coffee," Grandmother said, and motioned for me to come with her. We were on our way upstairs when we heard the door creak again.

"More people are coming," she said.

I stuck my head over the railing to try to see who it was, but I couldn't. It was dark in the hallway, and terrifying shadows with shifting shapes slipped along the walls, as in a nightmare.

We went up two flights, and Grandmother lit the fire in the winter room. I got back into bed.

Outside, the storm howled, and the rooftop chimneys groaned like living things. I began to wonder if the foundations of our house, instead of standing on solid ground, weren't paddling in the treacherous black water of the cistern.

These are bad times, dearie, we're living in a time of trouble and treachery . . . As sleep overcame me to the soothing rumble of brewing coffee, bits and pieces of conversation, words picked up here and there from adults, came to mind, their meanings as slippery as water.

When I woke up, the house seemed mute. Papa and Mamma were sleeping. I got up without making a sound and looked at the clock. It was nine in the morning. I went to my grandmother's room, but she was sleeping, too. It was the first time nobody had been awake at that hour.

The storm was over. I went to the living-room windows and looked out. Motionless grey clouds covered the high, cold sky. They looked as if they were stuck. Maybe the water they had bailed out of the cistern the night before had now evaporated and risen up into the clouds to frown sternly down at the wet roofs and gloomy earth.

The first thing I noticed when I looked down at the lower part of town was that the river had overflowed. Not surprising, in weather like that. It must have tried all night, as usual, to jump over the bridge, shaking it like a pack-horse trying to throw off a painful load. You could see the mark of the river's wild nocturnal efforts most clearly on its bloody back. Having failed to sweep away the bridge, the river had turned on the road and swallowed it whole. Immensely swollen from this gulp, the river was now busy digesting the road. But the road was tough, accustomed to these unexpected attacks, and now lay patiently under the swirling reddish waters, waiting for them to withdraw.

Stupid river, I thought. Every winter it tries to bite the city's feet. But it wasn't as dangerous as it looked. The torrents that spilled down from the mountains were a lot worse. They too, like the river, tried to bite. But while the river would strut haughtily at the city's feet before its attack, the torrents rushing down the gullies leapt treacherously on its back. The gullies were usually empty. They looked like dead, dried-out snakes strewn across the mountainside. But on stormy nights they came to life, puffed themselves up, hissed and roared. And down they hurtled, pale with anger, with their dog-like names — Cullo, Fico, Cfakë — rolling chunks of earth and rock down from the higher sections of the city.

I looked out at the countryside, transformed during the night, and thought that if the river hated the bridge, the road surely felt the same hatred for the river, and the torrents for the embankments and the wind for the mountain that checked its fury. And they all must have loathed the wet, grey city that looked down with contempt on this destructive hatred. But I loved the city most of all because it stood alone against the others in this war.

Without taking my eyes off the roofs, I tried to understand what connection there might have been between last night's storm and Çeço Kaili's daughter, whose beard of bad omen suddenly came back to mind. Then my thoughts turned to the cistern. I got up and went downstairs. The hall was drenched. The buckets and ropes had been left in a heap on the floor. Somehow they made the hallway seem even more silent. I walked to the mouth of the cistern, lifted the lid, and leaned in.

"A-oo," I said to it quietly, as if afraid to rouse some monster.

"A-oo," answered the cistern almost reluctantly, in a hoarse, strange voice. I knew then that its anger had subsided, but not completely, for its voice was more muffled than usual.

I went back up the two flights to the living room, looked out and saw with joy that far off, at a distance too great to measure, a rainbow had appeared, like a brand-new peace treaty between mountain, river, bridge, torrents, road, wind and city. But it was easy to see that the truce would not last very long.

"OK, you can have France and Canada, but give me Luxembourg."

"You're kidding! You really want Luxembourg?"

"If it's all right with you."

"Well, give me Abyssinia for two Polands, and we could make a deal."

"No, not Abyssinia. Take France and Canada for two Polands."

"No way!"

"All right, then, give me back the India I gave you yesterday for Venezuela."

"India? Here, it's yours. What do I want with India anyway? To tell you the truth, I changed my mind about it last night."

"Did you also change your mind about Turkey, by any chance?"

"I already sold Turkey. Otherwise, I'd give it back to you."

"In that case, you don't get the Germany I promised you yesterday. I'd rather tear it up."

"Big deal. You think I care?"

We had been haggling for an hour, sitting in the middle of the street trading stamps. We were still arguing when Javer came by. He said, "Still carving up the world, I see."

II

Xhexho and Kako Pino had come to visit. They sat on a sofa in the living room, sipped coffee and chatted with Grandmother. Xhexho was worried. Grandmother seemed calmer, but she too looked uneasy. Kako Pino, frail and dressed all in black, kept shaking her small head with its thin, drawn face, repeating hypnotically after Xhexho's every word, "It's the end of the world." I was captivated by what they were saying. They were talking about Isa, Mane Voco's older son, who had done something unheard of last week: he had started wearing glasses.

"When they first told me," Xhexho said, "I couldn't believe my ears. I got up, threw a scarf on my head, and went to see Mane Voco. The poor man was taking it bravely, but the women of the house looked stunned, as if they'd been turned to stone. I wanted to ask them what was going on, but I couldn't. How can you speak of something like that? Well, who should walk in at that very moment? Isa, his glasses flashing! 'How are you? How's everything?' he says to me, just like that. Well, I wanted the ground to swallow me up. There was a lump in my throat. How I kept from bursting into tears, I'm sure I don't know. He walked over to the cabinet, flipped through a few books, then went over to the window, stopped, and took off his glasses. Then he started rubbing his eyes. His mother and sisters stared at him, their lips trembling. I reached out, picked up the glasses, and put them on. What can I tell you, my friends? My head was spinning. These glasses must be cursed. The world whirled like the circles of hell. Everything shook, rolled and swayed as if possessed by the devil. I took them off in a hurry, and got up and ran out like a madwoman."

Xhexho took a deep breath. Grandmother turned her coffee cup upside down to read the grains.

"Why did Isa do it?" she said sadly. "Such a quiet, intelligent boy. With a lout like Lame Kareco Spiri, I could understand it, but Isa . . ."

"The end of the world," said Kako Pino.

"That's the way it is, Selfixhe," Xhexho went on. "We complain about all the evils that befall us, but we have only ourselves to blame. Yesterday they built a house of cardboard, today the boys wear glasses, and tomorrow, who can say? But the Almighty above," and here Xhexho pointed a finger at the ceiling and her tone became menacing, "sees all and records all. He'll make us pay."

"The end of the world," said Kako Pino again.

When Xhexho mentioned the cardboard house, I instinctively turned towards the Gjobek district, where the strange breeze-block construction, put up a few weeks ago by the Italians for their nuns, now stood — an alien structure quite incompatible with the sober stone houses all around it. This unusual building bothered people for a long time. We've never seen anything like this, said old women who knew the ways of the world and had even been to Turkey. Old as we are, we have never heard of a cardboard house before. It's the devil's work, for sure.

They now judged Mane Voco's son in more or less the same terms as they had applied to the breeze-block house. "Why, dreadful boy, do you want to see the world except as it is? Why do you rebel?"

They discussed the matter endlessly, and I listened carefully, because what Mane Voco's son had done had something to do with a secret of mine. I too had put one of those accursed lenses to my eye more than once. I had found it in Grandmother's old chest, and playing with it one day I happened to raise it to one eye. I was astonished. Suddenly the world around me fell into place. The edges of things suddenly got sharper and brighter. I sat for a long time holding the lens over one eye and closing the other, looking out at the wide view from our house. It was amazing, as if an invisible hand had wiped clean a misted window that had covered the world, revealing it as something new and bright. Despite that, I didn't like it. I was used to looking at the world through a cloud of haze, so that the edges of things ran together and separated freely, not according to any fixed rules. No one, I reckoned, asked the roofs, streets or telegraph poles to account for slight shifts from their starting positions. But through that round glass the world looked stiff, measured and mean, granting objects no more qualities than those they already had. It was like a house where everything — oil, flour, even water — was measured to the last drop and nothing was ever left over or accidentally spilled.

All the same, the lens came in very handy at the movies. Before I went I would wash it and put it in my pocket. When the lights went out I would take it out, close my left eye, and put it over my right. When I got home no one could understand why one of my eyes was a little red. One night, two gypsy kids I'd taken with me to see the film got very curious when I took out the lens. During the film I heard them whispering to each other "D'you reckon he be a spy?"

"The end of the world," Kako Pino said again.

But they soon went back to their usual boring conversation about the cost of living. I wasn't interested, so I started wondering again why people see with their eyes and not with their fingers, cheeks or some other part of the body. Eyes, after all, were only pieces of flesh from our bodies. How does the world manage to get in through an eye? Why don't people blow up from the great mass of light, space and colour that constantly pours into them through their eyes? I had racked my brains for a long time over the enigma of sight. I was obsessed by the mystery of blindness, which I feared more than anything else. This fear may have come from the fact that most of the curses I used to hear had to do with eyes. Once our toilet was blocked, and the dark hole of the drain looked to me like a blind eye. That must be how eyes get stopped up, I said to myself. The flow of light, with all those sights dissolved in it, can't get through the eye sockets, and that must be what blindness is. Vehip Qorri, the town poet, must have just that kind of liquid blackness in his eye sockets.

Sight. What an inexplicable thing! I turn my head towards the lower sections of the city and my eyes, like two great pumps, start sucking in the light with all those images of roofs, chimneys, a few lone fig trees, streets, passers-by. Can they feel me sucking them in? I close my eyes. The flow stops. I open them. It starts again.

After the stormy night, the roofs seemed to have come unusually close to one another. They were soaking wet. The stone slates formed an infuriatingly monotonous expanse as far as I could see. The light glanced off them, casually. Down below, streets and alleys twisted and turned, with only a handful of people to be seen on them: a few peasants on horseback, a priest, old women dressed in black, out visiting.

Varosh Street crept painfully uphill alongside the gullies, while on its right Gjobek Street plunged down steeply, skirting the Italian nuns' cardboard house as if it were plague-stricken, and then crashed into Varosh Street, a collision from which both streets emerged crooked. Further on, Fools' Alley, blind and obstinate, lurched towards genteel Gymnasium Street, which dodged it at the last minute with a clever twist. Then Fools' Alley, as if looking for trouble with other streets, tumbled around the district with sudden, sharp turns.

I was watching out for Ilir, my best friend, Mane Voco's younger son, to come round the corner. When I saw him I ran downstairs and into the street.

"Let's go over to the slaughterhouse," he said. "We've never done that before."

"The slaughterhouse? What for?"

"What do you mean, what for? To watch. To see how they kill the cows and sheep."

"What's to see at the slaughterhouse? We've seen the butcher shops. Carcasses hanging on hooks, some with their legs up, some with them down."

"Butchers' shops are one thing," Ilir said, "but slaughtering is another. There are no tiresome customers haggling over the price of meat. You can even see them kill bulls. All they do there is kill animals."

"Slaughter" was one of the words being bandied about more and more often, but its meaning still seemed rather vague.

"Last week," Ilir went on, "a bull escaped from the meat-packers and ran wild. They all chased after him and hit him with anything they could get their hands on until finally he fell off the steps and broke his back. A lot of grown-ups go just to watch."

To be honest, the places in the city where you could see anything of interest could be counted on the fingers of one hand. Apart from the movies, which were for children and the frivolous, there were only two places you might get to see a fight, usually on Sundays: the gypsy district and the square behind the mosque, where the porters divided up their earnings. Other fights were accidental and usually broke out in unpredictable places. And recently a lot of fights had not lived up to the pre-match invective. More than once I had heard onlookers complain, "Bah, in our day they knew how to break bones," and then walk off disappointed. Only the Gypsies and the porters really fought hard and kept almost all the promises they'd made prior to the fight.

The slaughterhouse seemed to be a new amusement, so I didn't argue.

As we trudged up the cobblestone street, we saw Javer and Maksut, Nazo's boy, coming down. They weren't talking to each other and looked cross. We didn't say anything either. Maksut had always had eyes that bulged out of their sockets, and I didn't like looking at him. One day I heard a woman arguing with a neighbour, and when she screamed "May your eyes burst from their sockets," I thought of Nazo's boy right away, and now every time I saw him I felt that his eyes might pop out and roll along the cobblestones and I might accidentally step on them and burst them open.

"What's the matter?" asked Ilir. "What's the frown for?"

"It's Nazo's boy. When I see him it turns my stomach."

"Isa doesn't like him either," Ilir said. "Whenever his name is mentioned, Isa frowns just the way you did."

"Really? So Isa thinks his eyes are going to pop out too?"

"Are you crazy?"

I let it drop.

There was a man coming towards us down the street, draped in a blanket, carrying a lump of bread wrapped in a piece of cloth. It was Llukan, whom people called The Shadow.

"So, you're out of jail!" a passer-by said to him.

"Yes, I'm out."

"When are you going back?"

"And why shouldn't I go back? Prisons are made for men."

Since the days of the Turks, Llukan had been in prison dozens of times for petty crimes. Everyone always remembered him trudging down the street from the citadel in just that way, with a brown blanket over his shoulders and in his hand some meagre victuals wrapped in a handkerchief.

"So, Llukan, you're out again!" someone else said.

"Sure am, friend."

"You could have left the blanket up there. You'll be back soon enough."

Llukan responded with a flood of insults. The further away he went, the louder he shouted.

We walked towards the centre of town. The streets were full of alien sounds. It was market day. Peasants from all over were converging on the square. Horseshoes clacked, slid and sparked on the cobblestones. On the hills villagers drew their horses by the bridles, their sweating, panting bodies merging with those of their animals as they dragged them upwards.

The windows of the great houses were shut tight on both sides of the street. Behind them the wives of the agas sat on soft cushions and held their noses, felt faint, and nearly vomited, complaining about the stench of the peasants wafting in from the street. Plump, with white round faces, they rarely ventured out into the city. They protested that the closing of the border with Greece had kept them from getting the eels from Lake Ioannina that were so good for their rheumatism. They found the peasants repugnant and never mentioned them without first muttering "excuse the expression," as they did when saying the word "lavatory." In fact, they were dismayed by the times they lived in, and sat in rows on their cushions sipping coffee endlessly and yearning for the return of the monarchy.

Some Italian soldiers stood guard at the cinema, watching people go by. We carried on up the street. The shop signs stretched out one after another. Tinsmith. Barber. Addis Ababa Café. Saddles. Vinegar. And a poster that began with the words "I order" in big letters.

We walked on until the slaughterhouse was near. You still couldn't hear the bleating of the sheep or smell the blood, and there was no sign, but somehow it was clear that the slaughterhouse was nearby. The silent cobblestones and deserted street corner told us that we were close to it. We started up a slippery wet stairway, not at all like a set of ordinary stone steps. It was very high and its risers bore none of the carvings or decorations we were used to, not even simple ones. It was a hard climb. There was a tomb-like silence at the top. Not a sound made by man or beast. What were they doing up there? Finally we arrived. Everything was ready. The men standing around waiting nonchalantly were well dressed, with white shirts, stiff collars and neckties. Some of them wore soft felt Borsalino hats. One had an old-fashioned top hat. He looked at his watch.

We heard a splash of water. A man was watering the ground with a black rubber hose. Another man with a broom swept the water into the gutters at the side. Water splattered near our feet. We looked down and stepped back, but it was too late. The ground was full of blood. Everything must have been done before we got there. But no one made a move to leave, so they must have been getting ready for another killing. The water foamed over the broad puddles of blood, washing them from the cement pavement, and carrying them away before they could harden.

Then we saw everything. The rectangular yard was ringed on all sides by a one-storey building, also in cement. A hundred iron hooks hung from the ceiling. Below there were sheep, and among them peasants in thick black wool cloaks, bending over the backs of the animals, clutching them by their wool. They too were waiting.

The group of spectators seemed in no hurry. Two of them

had taken out their strings of beads and were slowly ticking them off. I had never seen them before. The one with the top hat looked at his watch. Apparently it was time.

Suddenly we saw the slaughterers, with their white coats and chapped, sinewy hands. They were standing near the fountain at the centre of the square, and they remained motionless even when the peasants began pushing the animals towards them from the stalls. There was a muffled rumble as thousands of hooves scuffed the ground. It was a low, rhythmic noise, and it went on for a long time. When the first animals drew near the fountain where the slaughterers were waiting, we suddenly saw the gleam of the knives. Then it began.

I felt a pain in my right hand. Ilir's nails were sinking into my flesh. I felt sick.

"Let's go."

Neither of us actually spoke those words, but we sought the stairs blindly, with our hands over our eyes.

At last we found them, ran down as fast as we could, and were off. The farther we got from the slaughterhouse, the livelier the streets were. People were going home from the market, laden with produce. Others were just on their way there. Did they have any idea what was going on in the slaughterhouse?

"Where have you been?" a voice suddenly thundered, seeming to roll from the sky. We looked up. It was Mane Voco, Ilir's father, standing in front of us. He was holding a loaf of bread and a bunch of fresh onions.

"Where have you been?" he asked again. "Why are you so pale?"

"We were up there . . . at the slaughterhouse."

"The slaughterhouse?" The onions writhed in his hand like snakes. "What were you doing at the slaughterhouse?"

"Nothing, Papa, just watching."

"Watching what?"

The onions stopped moving; their stalks hung limply. "I don't want you going up there again," Mane Voco said in a milder tone. His fingers searched for something in his vest pocket. Finally he came up with half a lek. "Here," he said, "go to the movies, both of you."

He left. Gradually we recovered from the shock. The sights of the market comforted us as we walked through it. On counters, in baskets, sacks and unfolded kerchiefs lay a world of green that couldn't be found in our part of the city: cabbage, onions, lettuce, milk, fresh eggs, cheese, parsley. And in the midst of it all, the clinking of coins. Questions and answers. "How much?" "How much!" Murmurings. Curses. "May you drop dead before you eat them!" "This'll pay for your doctor." So much poison flowed over the lettuces and cabbages! Where worms crawled, there crept death . . . "And how much is that?"

We walked on. At the far end of the market, an Italian soldier sat playing a harmonica and making eyes at the girls. We were back at the cinema. There was no film that day.

We went home. On my way upstairs, I heard my youngest aunt laughing. She was sitting on a chair, jiggling one leg and laughing loudly. Xhexho looked over to Grandmother two or three times, but she only pursed her lips as if to say, "What can you do, Xhexho? That's how girls act these days."

My father came in. "Did you hear?" my aunt said to him at once. "They took a shot at the King of Italy in Tirana."

"I heard at the coffee house," my father said. "The assassin had hidden his pistol in a bouquet of roses."

"Really?"

"They're going to hang him tomorrow. He's only seventeen."

"Oh, the poor boy," Grandmother sighed.

"The end of the world."

"Too bad he didn't get him," my aunt shouted out. "The roses got in his way."

"Where do you hear such things?" my mother asked in a tone of reproach.

"Here and there," was all my aunt would say.

Xhexho adjusted the kerchief on her head, said goodbye to Grandmother and Kako Pino, and left. Kako Pino left soon after. My aunt stayed on for a while.

I went up the two flights. There was still some activity in the streets. The last people were going home from the market. Maksut, Nazo's boy, was carrying a cabbage that looked like a severed head. He seemed to be smiling broadly.

The peasants had started packing up. Soon their black cloaks would darken the streets — Varosh, Palorto, Hazmurat, Çetemel, Zall — and the highway and bridge, too, as they made their way back to the villages that we never saw. The city, like a tethered horse, would swallow up the greenery they had brought. But all that soft green, that meadow dew and tinkle of cowbells, was not enough to soften the city's harshness. They were leaving now, their black cloaks dancing in the twilight. The cobblestones flashed their last sparks of anger under the iron horseshoes. It was getting late. The peasants had to hurry home to their villages. They never even turned to look back at the city, alone now with its stones. A muffled ringing rolled down the hill from the citadel. Every evening the guards checked the window bars, striking them rhythmically with iron rods.

I saw the last of the peasants crossing the bridge over the river and I thought about the strange division of people into peasants and city-dwellers. What were the villages like? Where were they and why didn't we ever see them? To tell the truth I didn't really believe the villages existed. It seemed to me that the peasants were only pretending to go to their villages, while actually they weren't going anywhere, just crouching behind the scattered bush-covered hillocks around the city, waiting out the long week for another market day, when once again they would fill the streets with greens, eggs and the tinkling of bells.

I wondered how it was that it had occurred to people to pile up so many stones and so much wood to make all those walls and roofs and then call that great heap of streets, roofs, chimneys and yards a city. But even less comprehensible were the words "occupied city," which came up more and more in the grown-ups' conversations. Our city was occupied. Which meant that there were foreign soldiers in it. That much I knew, but there was something else that bothered me. I couldn't see how a city could be unoccupied. And anyway, even if our city wasn't occupied, wouldn't there be these same streets, the same fountains, roofs and people? Wouldn't I still have the same mother and father and wouldn't Xhexho, Kako Pino, Aunt Xhemo and all the same people still come to visit?

"You can't understand what a free city means, because you're growing up in slavery," Javer told me one day when I asked him about it. "It's hard to explain it to you, believe me, but in a free city, everything will be so different, so beautiful, that at first we'll all be dazzled."

"Will we get a lot to eat?"

"Of course we'll eat. But there'll be lots of other things besides eating. So many things that I don't even know them all myself."

From time to time the sun shone through the clouds. The rain fell in sparse drops that seemed to smile secretly. The wooden door opened, and Kako Pino went out into the street. Skinny, dressed all in black, holding the red bag with her instruments under her arm, she set out nimbly down the street. The rain fell lightly, joyfully. There was a wedding somewhere, and Kako Pino was going. Her wizened hands, drawing various objects out of her bag — tweezers, hairpins, thread, boxes — decorated the brides' faces with star-like dots, cypress branches and signs of the zodiac, all floating in the white mystery of powder.

I exhaled lightly on the windowpane, fogging up the image of Kako Pino. All I could see was a black shape waddling at the far end of the street. Some day she would go out like that to make up my bride. Could you paint a rainbow on her face, Kako Pino? I had been wondering about that for a long time.

But now she had turned into another street, where she looked even smaller among the intolerably tall houses. Behind the heavy doors, with their solid iron fittings, were the beautiful young brides.

FRAGMENT OF A CHRONICLE

we met again, this time in Nuremberg. The happy news had just been announced. Ettore Muti, secretary of the Fascist Party and a great friend of Albania, would soon be visiting our region. Our city is preparing a fitting reception. Trial. Executive orders. Property. The body of our fellow citizen L. Xuano was fished out of the river. Killed when he was supposed to appear as a witness in the Angonis' suit against the Karllashi family. The case, which has been going on for sixty years now, has done great harm to our city. It has been discovered that Ahmet Zogu, the sultan of Albania, the Ogre, bought a palace in Vienna for two million leks as a gift for his mistress, Mizzi. The heaviest person in the city right now is Aqif Kashahu, who weighs 159 kilos. The troublesome elements have been expelled from the secondary school. All citizens possessing arms without permits are to report to the command post. The seventeenth of this month is the deadline. Bruno Arcivocale commanding. Our fellow citizen Bido Sherifi returned yesterday from Tirana, where he spent ten days. Births. Marriages. Deaths. To A. Dhrami and to Z. Bashari was born a boy, to M. Xhiku a girl. N. Fico married E. Karafili,

III

A number of things happened in the city that seemed unrelated at first. A veiled woman was seen fiddling with something on the ground at the last crossroads on the street leading to the citadel. Then she sprinkled the place with water and left quickly, getting away from the people who tried to follow her. An unknown old woman was seen under a window of Nazo's house, where her young daughter-in-law was cutting her nails. The old woman gathered up the nail clippings in the street and went off cackling to herself. Bido Sherifi woke up suddenly in the middle of the night, crowed two or three times like a rooster, and went back to sleep. The next morning he claimed he remembered nothing. Two days later Kako Pino found a pile of damp ashes in her yard. But everything became clear after what happened to Mane Voco's wife. Then no one could say that these events were unrelated, as had been thought at first. One day, towards noon, a dark-skinned woman knocked at Mane Voco's door and asked for a glass of water. The lady of the house brought it for her, but the stranger drank only half of it. As Mane Voco's wife held out her hand to take back the glass, the unknown woman suddenly said, "Why do you give me water in a dirty glass?," and threw what was left of it in her face. Mane Voco's poor wife turned pale with fear. Then the visitor vanished in the twinkling of an eye. Mane Voco's wife quickly put a cauldron on the fire, bathed from head to foot, and burned the clothes she had been wearing.

Now it was obvious: witchcraft was rampant throughout town. Invisible hands scattered evil objects everywhere: under doorsteps, behind walls, under eaves, wrapped in old papers or dirty rags that made you shudder. People said that a spell had been cast on the house of the Cutes, where the brothers hated each other and the quarrelling was endless. The same happened to the house of Dino Çiço, the city's lone inventor, whose calculations were now thrown off by the magic. Furthermore, the behaviour of certain young girls in recent days could be explained only as a consequence of the practice of witchcraft.

In our house, we were waiting for Xhexho. And come she did, breathing heavily as always, her nasal voice booming as she walked through the gate. "Have you heard, poor things?" she called from the steps. "Babaramo's daughter-in-law's milk has run dry."

"God help us," my mother said, going green in the face.

"You should see what happened there. They looked all over for the magic ball, on the ceiling, under the floorboards. They turned over the mattresses, emptied all the chests. They turned the whole house upside down until they finally found it."

"They found it?"

"They did. Right in the baby's cradle: nails and hair of the dead. You should have seen them! Wailing and crying. They kept it up until the oldest son came home and went to tell the police."

"It's the work of witches," my mother said. "Why can't they find them?"

"Has anything happened at your place?" asked Xhexho.

"No," said Grandmother. "Not so far."

"That's good."

"Witches," my mother kept repeating.

"What about Nazo's boy?" Xhexho asked. "Have they managed to get rid of his curse?"

"Not yet," said Grandmother. "They called the hodja twice but nothing yet. They've turned the house upside down looking for the magic, but they can't find it."

"Too bad," said Xhexho. "Such a good-looking boy!"

I had heard about this business with Maksut, Nazo's son. He had been married just a short time when the rumour started that a spell had done something to him. Ilir had heard about it at home and told us. We were very curious to find out what was going on in that house which had been struck by a spell. Not until much later did I understand that it had affected Maksut's performance of his conjugal duties. We would sit by their door for hours, but it seemed that nothing unusual ever happened. Behind the windows everything was as quiet as it had always been. Nazo and her daughter-in-law still hung the clothes out to dry in the yard and the grey tomcat invariably lay on the roof, warming itself in the sun.

"What kind of spell is this?" we asked each other. "No screaming. No hair-pulling."

One day I asked Grandmother, "What is this spell on Nazo's boy?"

"Listen," Grandmother said, "these are shameful things you shouldn't talk about at your age. Understand?"

I told my friends, and they got even more curious. In the evening, when the hodja was praying in the mosque and the storks' nests atop the chimneys and minarets looked like black turbans, we went to wait outside Nazo's house to see the young bride. She came out and sat with her mother-in-law on a stone bench near the door. Her fingers toyed with her long braids and a strange, fascinating light flashed in her eyes now and then. Our neighbourhood had never seen such a splendid bride. Among ourselves we called her "the beautiful bride," and we liked it when she looked at us as we ran past Nazo's front door chasing fireflies in the twilight. She would sit there, watching us with her big grey eyes, but her mind seemed elsewhere. Then Maksut would come home from the market or the coffee house carrying a big loaf of bread under his arm. The bride and her mother-in-law would get up silently from the stone bench and he would follow them inside, closing the heavy door, which creaked plaintively behind him.

Behind that stone threshold, the spell must have been working. We felt sorry for the beautiful bride who disappeared every night behind that grim door. The street seemed empty, and we didn't feel like playing any more. Through the window we watched Nazo light the kerosene lamp, whose dim yellow light would have depressed anyone.

"Yes, Selfixhe," said Xhexho, "it's all our own fault. People have just gone too far. They say that in a few days all the men and women of the city are going to parade through the streets with flags and music, shouting 'Long live shit!' Has anyone ever seen such an abomination?"

Mother pinched her cheeks, which was a way of saying how upset she was.

"It's the end of the world!"

"How disgraceful! How disgraceful!" Grandmother said.

"Who knows what's next?" said Xhexho. "But He on high," she went on, pointing up as she always did, "He may take His time, but He never forgets. Yesterday He made Çeço Kaili's daughter grow a beard, tomorrow He will make all our bodies sprout thorns."

"God save us!" my mother cried.

Before she left, Xhexho gave us some advice. Whenever she gave advice, her voice got even more nasal. "When you cut your nails, don't leave the clippings around. Burn them, so nobody can find them."

"Why?"

"Because they use nail clippings for witchcraft, boy. And you, my girl, I beg you, when you comb your hair, be careful not to leave any tufts around, because the devil lies in wait for just such things."

"God save us!" my mother said once again.

"And bury the ashes from the fireplace too!"

Xhexho left as she had come, wrapped in black, and still wheezing. She left fear and unease in her wake, as she always did. That's how I remember her, always agitated and consumed with worry, never talking about anything pleasant, only about dark things, seemingly invigorated by them. Ilir suspected her of practising magic and casting spells herself.

Magic was now the constant topic of conversation in every home. In the beginning, after the first events, there was a kind of perplexity. Then, as is usual in such cases, once the uncertainty had passed, people started looking for the root of the evil, for the cause. The "old crones" were consulted. These

were aged women who could never be surprised or frightened
by anything any more. They had long since stopped going out
of their houses, for they found the world boring. To them even
major events like epidemics, floods and wars were only repe-
titions of what they had seen before. They had already been
old ladies in the thirties, under the monarchy, and even before,
under the republic in the mid-twenties. In fact, they were old
during the First World War and even before, at the turn of
the century. Granny Hadje had not been out of her house in
twenty-two years. One old woman of the Zeka family had been
inside for twenty-three years. Granny Neslihan had last gone
out thirteen years before, to bury her last grandson. Granny
Shano spent thirty-one years inside until one day she went out
into the street a few yards in front of her house to assault an
Italian officer who was making eyes at her great-granddaughter.
These crones were very robust, all nerve and bone, even though
they ate very little and smoked and drank coffee all day long.
When Granny Shano grabbed the Italian officer by the ear,
he let out a great yelp, drew his pistol, and rapped the old
woman's hand with the butt. Not only did she refuse to let go,
she punched him with her bony hands. The crones had very
little flesh on their bones, and few vulnerable spots. Their
bodies were like corpses ready for embalming, from which all
innards likely to rot had already been removed. Superfluous
emotions like curiosity, fear and lust for gossip or excitement
had been shed along with the useless flesh and excess fat. Javer
once said that Granny Shano could as easily have grabbed the
ear of Benito Mussolini himself as the Italian officer's.

The old crones gave very sober advice about the practice of witchcraft. They suggested that outbreaks of magic

usually occurred on the eve of great events, when people's spirits flutter like leaves before a storm.

Many questions remained, including the most important: who were the practitioners of witchcraft? But people didn't simply ask questions, they also took steps. Aqif Kashahu's boys stood guard day and night, in shifts, hiding in a dormer window. Kako Pino, who in her capacity as make-up woman for the city's brides was one of the most vulnerable targets of magic, bought a huge wolf-like dog and let it run loose in her yard.

Mane Voco brought his ancient rifle, a relic from the days of Turkish rule, up from the cellar and he kept it to hand, hanging on a nail behind the door. The mayor's office posted an extra guard in the city cemetery.

People took certain other precautionary measures, too. Housewives kept the ash from the fireplace in the cupboard, under lock and key, as if it was flour. Men leaving the barbershop carried their clipped hair and shavings wrapped up in a rag or a piece of newspaper. These precautions seemed to stem the flow of sorcery. The ordinary concerns of daily life, which had disappeared from conversation because of the magic, began to crop up again. Some sense of security and tranquillity returned. But it didn't last. Just when it seemed that the evil spells had gone for good, they attacked again with unexpected fury. Their return was signalled by the explosion of a sealed barrel of cheese, which made a terrific noise when it blew up in the middle of the night at the house of Avdo Babaramo, the former gunner. In response to this new outbreak of witchcraft, the mayor's office posted notices around the city urging people to help apprehend those responsible. But this didn't work. Murky misdeeds went on being done. One night, someone smiled at Aqif Kashahu's wife from a dormer window, making a come-hither gesture. After the explosion of the cheese barrel, Avdo Babaramo's elder son, so it was said, became estranged from his wife. But it was the third incident, directed against Kako Pino, that caused the greatest uproar. The evil omen itself was nothing very unusual — on the contrary, ashes again, but this time sprinkled with vinegar. The trouble was that the clamour we kids made when we saw how shaken Kako Pino was on discovering the magic attracted the attention of an Italian patrol that happened to be passing by at the time. The patrol must have reported the unusual agitation to the garrison, because a quarter of an hour later four Italian sappers trooped into Kako Pino's yard with mine detectors. They looked at our frightened eyes, saw Kako Pino scratching her own face from fear, and, without asking for any explanation, began searching the spot all of us were staring at.

"Hell," one of them kept saying over and over, "the detector says there's nothing here."

A few minutes later they stalked off angrily, and as they moved down the street one of them shouted back at Kako Pino, "*Che puttana!*"

Every evening now, as night drew near, our heads were filled with thoughts of magic. This was understandable, for when the night enveloped everything, from the citadel and its prison at the top of the hill right down to the stony river bed at the bottom, somewhere in the deserted alleyways unseen hands were collecting hair and nail clippings, chimney soot and other dark matter, wrapping them in scraps of cloth, and whispering spells to make your blood run cold.

The proud and sullen city, having defied rain, hail,

thunder and rainbows, now gnawed at itself. The stretching of the eaves, the warped twisting of the streets, the strange position of the chimneys all testified to its torment.

"The city is sick." It was the second time I had heard those words. I couldn't understand how a city could be ill. In Mane Voco's yard, Ilir and I listened to Javer and Isa talking about witchcraft. As usual when they talked among themselves, they used difficult and unknown words, the sound of which seemed ill suited to a discussion of matters that were already mysterious enough. Several times we heard them use the words "mysticism" and "collective psychosis." Then Isa asked Javer, "Have you read Jung?"

"No," said Javer. "And I have no intention to do so either."

"I came across one of his books by accident. He discusses this very question."

"What do I care about Jung?" said Javer. "All this is clear enough. This psychosis serves the interests of the reactionaries by diverting public attention from the real problems. Here, look at the newspaper: 'Magic is in some sense part of a nation's traditional folklore.'"

"A fascist theory," Isa said.

Javer tossed the paper aside.

"Those barbarians with feathers in their hats are happy to resurrect any medieval custom, as long as Mussolini can get something out of it."

Javer had been expelled from the secondary school two weeks before for having taken part in acts of violence against an Italian teacher. He was now working in Mak Karllashi's tannery.

He took a small piece of paper out of his pocket and scribbled on it in his slanted handwriting: "Forget about this idiotic magic. We have other things to worry about."

"Not bad," said Isa, polishing his glasses, "but maybe it would be better if we explained it a little more scientifically."

Javer scowled, but not for long. The two friends finally noticed that we had been listening to them.

"Hey, you ghost-hunters! Have you been spying on us?"

The truth was that, like most kids in the neighbourhood, we were always on the lookout for magic talismans. We spent entire days searching everywhere: under doorsteps, in old cabinets, on roofs, in the bottom of fireplaces. Traces of our searches could be seen everywhere, and were especially apparent when it rained and the roof slates we had moved let in leaks. We had concentrated our investigations around Nazo's house, because of her beautiful daughter-in-law.

Despite all our efforts, we had not found a single talisman, and we never imagined that we would discover one just when we had finally given up all hope.

It happened one sunny day in Fools' Alley. We wouldn't have traded this crooked ugly alley for any boulevard in the world, because no great street would ever have been so generous as to let children peel off its cobbles in broad daylight and do whatever they wanted with them. But Fools' Alley, crazy as it was, allowed us to do that.

That day we were playing at throwing stones, when suddenly someone shouted in fear: "Look at this!"

We all ran towards him, then stopped, petrified. His face was tinged with green as he pointed to a dark spot on the ground. There among the rocks lay a magic ball the size of a fist. We cast frightened glances at one another, and words stuck in our throats. (Xhexho later told me that the magic had stolen our power of speech.) But then suddenly great courage came upon us, as sometimes happens in a dream when you find yourself alone in some dark, deserted street, and your heart pounds in fright, and you sense that something evil is going to happen in this strange street, and you wait and wait for the evil, but it holds back, and you wait some more, and your fear mounts, and then somewhere something moves, and a shadow, a half-seen face, comes near, and your knees buckle, and your voice goes, and you're about to faint, but then suddenly, at the last minute, some insane fury grips you, and your limbs feel free, and your voice booms like thunder, and you cry out, you charge the ghost, and you . . . wake up. And that's what happened to us.

"The magic! The magic!" we all yelled. Ilir picked it up and carried it off

"Witchcraft, witchcraft!" I yelled along with the others, and without knowing why, we raced down the alley, Ilir in the lead. We charged after him, screaming and panting in a mixture of joy and horror.

Shutters flew open noisily, and women young and old stuck their heads out in terror. "What is it? What's going on?"

"The magic! The magic!" we howled, thundering through the neighbourhood like a pack of mad dogs.

Kako Pino appeared in her window and made the sign of the cross; Nazo's beautiful daughter-in-law smiled with her big eyes; Mane Voco poked the long barrel of his rifle out of the dormer; and Isa's face lit up behind the big lenses of his glasses, which shone like two suns.

"Ilir!" cried Mane Voco's wife, pinching her cheeks and lurching after us. "Ilir, my son, for the love of God throw it away! Throw it away!"

But Ilir paid no attention. His eyes bulging, he ran on, as we followed behind.

"The magic! The magic!"

Our mothers shouted to us from windows and doors and over garden walls. They clawed their cheeks in horror, threat-ened and wept, but still we ran on, refusing to abandon the magic object. We believed we held the city's anguish in that filthy ball of rags.

In the end we got tired and came to a stop at Zamani Square, bathed in sweat and covered with dust, barely able to catch our breath, but radiant with joy.

"What do we do now?" someone asked.

"Anyone have a match?"

Someone did.

Ilir lit the magic ball and threw it down. As it burned, we began to shout again, then unbuttoned our flies and pissed on it, cheering wildly and sprinkling each other for fun.

Water from the cistern wouldn't lather. "It's bewitched," said Xhexho. "Change it at once or you're done for."

Changing the water was a tough job. My father was reluctant. Grandmother insisted, and the other neighbourhood women who drew water from our cistern took her side. They collected some money and offered to work all day alongside the cleaning workers.

At last the decision was made. The chore began. The workers went up and down by rope, lamps in hand. Bucket after bucket was emptied. The old water came out to make way for the new.

Javer and Isa sat staring and smoking at the foot of the stairs, and burst out laughing from time to time.

"What's so funny?" asked Xhexho. "Why don't you get a bucket and give us a hand?"

"This great labour reminds us of the pyramids of Egypt," said Javer.

Nazo's daughter-in-law smiled.

The buckets were deafening as they clattered off the walls of the cistern.

"What we need is new people, not new water," Javer said. Isa burst out laughing.

Mane Voco, Isa's father, looked disapprovingly at the two boys.

Grandmother was coming down the stairs carrying a tray with cups of coffee for the workers.

Breathing hard, they sipped their coffee standing up. The lack of air deep in the cistern had made them pale. One of them was called Omer. When he went down, I leaned over the opening of the cistern and said his name.

"Omer," echoed the cistern. When it was empty, its voice was loud, but curiously hoarse, as though it had a cold.

"Do you know who Omer was — Homer, that is?" Isa asked me.

"No, tell me."

"He was a blind poet of ancient Greece."

"Who put out his eyes? The Italians?"

They laughed.

"He wrote wonderful books about one-eyed monsters and about a city called Troy and also about a wooden horse."

I leaned into the opening again. "Homer," I shouted. Patches of light and shadow mingled in the cistern.

"Hoooomer," it answered.

I thought I could hear the tapping of a blind man's cane.

FRAGMENT OF A CHRONICLE

while Japan prepared its attack on India and Australia. Trial.
Writ server. Property. Gole Balloma from the Varosh district
was subpoenaed for failure to pay his debts. L. Xuano's household goods will be auctioned on Sunday. Warrants have been
issued for the arrest of the old women H.Z. and C.V., charged
with practising magic. Readers are advised that the defective
quality of the last issue of the paper, with any errors that may
have crept in, was due to the stomach trouble from which I
suffered last week. Editor-in-chief. More undisciplined pupils
have been expelled from school. We have received a number
of complaints from parents about the teacher Qani Kekezi.
This gentleman's pedagogical procedures are strange indeed.
During anatomy lessons he dissects cats in front of the children, who are terrified. Recently a mutilated cat got loose
and leapt into the pupils' benches, trailing its intestines. Miss
Lejla Karllashi left yesterday for Italy. We take this opportunity to offer readers the departure times for the Durrës—Bari
steamship line. Addresses of the city's midwives.

IV

"You look a little sickly," Grandmother said. "You'd better go stay at your grandfather's for a few days."

I liked to visit our maternal grandfather, whom we called *Babazoti*. His was a more cheerful place, not so harsh, and most of all there was no hunger there as there was in our house. In our big house, maybe because of the hallways, cupboards and cellars, you could really feel the hunger. Besides, our neighbourhood was grey, thick with houses stuck almost on top of each other. Everything was hard and fixed, set down once and for all centuries ago. The streets, curves, corners, doorsteps, telephone poles and everything else seemed cut in stone and measured out to the last centimetre. But Grandfather's place was different. There was nothing rigid about it. Everything seemed soft and mobile. The ground was free to do as it pleased — to stay level, for example, or to hump its back and throw streams into the river like a donkey shaking off its load. The scenery had something human about it: as the seasons passed, it lost or gained weight, got lighter or darker, more beautiful or uglier. Whereas our neighbourhood was, so to speak, allergic to change.

47

Strangest of all was that that part of town had only two houses: Grandfather's and another about a hundred yards away. The wasteland between them was rough and unfriendly. On misty mornings, you sometimes saw a stoat dashing across it, but then for days on end it stayed empty. The snakes were getting ready to hibernate underground. The fallen rocks and stones, which had tumbled down from who knows where centuries ago and settled in the bushes and sparse grasses, added to the sense of desolation. Everyone considered it a part of the city that was dying. The paths across it varied their tracks, as if impatient to abandon the place forever. And the bushes became more and more daring, sprouting in the most unexpected places: in the middle of the street, alongside the fountain, in the courtyards. One had even tried to grow on a doorstep, and had paid for its temerity with its life.

The bushes were ominous. Wandering around with Ilir in the upper districts, along the border between the mountains and the city, I noticed that the brush had grown even behind the row of ruins of the last houses, long since abandoned. There they lurked like wild beasts, surrounding the whole city. At night I could hear them howling. It was a muffled howl, barely perceptible, almost like a sob.

On the north side was the road leading to the citadel and linking the city's upper districts with the centre. It overlooked the two houses at roof level. Once a truck had crashed into Babazoti's courtyard. Sometimes a drunk stumbled onto the roof and rain would drip in for a week. But it didn't happen often, since there were few passers-by on this street. From time to time somebody going home from the market in the hot afternoon would walk by singing at the top of his lungs.

The clock struck seven when I came by
I stood at your window and heaved a sigh.
And I heard what your darling voice said:
"If only I didn't have such a pain in my head."

It seemed that a woman named Miriam complained of recurring headaches at seven every evening. Not much to it, but I liked the song a lot. No one would have dared sing such a song in our neighbourhood. If anyone had, a dozen windows would be thrown open, and women young and old would claw their cheeks in shame and rain curses, and probably a bucket of water, down on the impertinent singer. But here, in this wide deserted space, you could shout to your heart's content and never fill it with the noise. It was no accident that the stranger broke into song as soon as he turned into this street. He must have been singing it in his head all day long, in the market, the coffee house, and the centre of town, eagerly waiting to get to this lonely place to let his lungs give full vent to it.

The evenings especially were stunningly beautiful in this neighbourhood, with a charm all their own. Whenever I heard people say "Good evening," I thought of Grandfather's courtyard, where the gypsies who lived in a separate shack would play their violins while Grandfather stretched out on a chaise longue and puffed on his big black pipe. The gypsies had not been able to pay their rent for years, and they seemed to consider these summer evening concerts a way of working off some of the debt.

"Babazoti," I would whisper, "roll me one, too," and without a word he'd roll a thin cigarette, light it and hand it to me. I'd sit beside him and suck on the burning tobacco in delight, ignoring the threatening gestures my aunts and uncles directed at me from the shadows.

I thought there was no greater happiness in the world than to sit smoking after a good meal, listening like Grandpa, with half-closed eyes, to the gypsies playing their violins.

Ah! I thought, when I grow up I'll buy myself a big black pipe that smokes like a chimney, and I'll grow a beard like Grandpa's and I'll lie on the divan and read great big books all day long.

"Babazoti," I said in a drawling, sleepy voice, "will you teach me Turkish?"

"I will," he answered, "when you're a little older." His voice was deep and soothing, and as I leaned against the chaise longue, I dreamed of the magic of tobacco and tried to figure out how much I would smoke and how many books I would have to read in Turkish before my time to die would come.

The thick books lay in the trunk, piled one on top of the other, an endless swarm of Arabic letters waiting to carry me off and reveal secrets and mysteries, for only Arabic letters knew the path to the mysteries, just as ants know the holes and fissures underground.

"Babazoti," I asked, "can you read ants?" He chuckled softly and patted my tousled hair.

"No, boy, you can't read ants."

"But why not? When they're all piled up together, they look just like Turkish letters."

"It only seems that way, but it's not really true."

"But I've seen them," I insisted one last time.

As I drew on my cigarette, I wondered what ants were for if you couldn't read them like books.

All these things were running pell-mell through my mind as I walked past Avdo Babaramo's house. He was an old artilleryman, whose house was the only one up near the citadel. Then I headed back down through the underbrush, along the narrow path that seemed to have moved one more time. Bits of memory, fragments of sentences or words, splinters of trivial events swarmed about, shoving and catching one another by the ear or nose with a brusqueness sharpened by the speed of my steps.

I came to Suzana's house. Once she heard I had come, she would run over and flutter around between the edge of the cliff and the gypsies' shack, where we'd played at skipping on my second visit. Then she would stop in the middle of the waste ground near a tree we called *badshade* and watch what was going on from afar. Then, for sure, she would creep close to the house, if she weren't feeling too fearful of Grandfather's Turkish books. Her flutterings had something of the butterfly but something of a stork as well. She was taller than me, thin, and had long hair that she combed in a different style each day. Everyone said she was pretty. There were no other little girls or boys in Grandfather's neighbourhood, so Suzana always waited impatiently for me to come. She said being around grown-ups bored her. Sitting at home embroidering bored her, going to the wash-house bored her, eating meals bored her. She was bored morning, noon and night. In short, she was *really* bored. She liked the word a lot and she spoke it with the greatest care, as if afraid to bruise it accidentally with tooth or tongue.

I would tell Suzana all kinds of things about life in our neighbourhood. She listened to everything attentively, with her eyebrows arched. Last time, when I told her about Çeço Kaili's daughter's beard, she opened her eyes wide, bit her lip two or three times, and was about to say something, but she held back, hesitated again, and then leaned forward, her face pale, her mouth near my ear, and asked: "Do you know any rude words?"

"Leave me alone, you idiot," I said.

"You're the one who's an idiot," she said, almost screaming, and ran off. As she ran she turned once and yelled from far off: "Idi-o-o-t!"

That evening she came back into the yard and, putting her long thin arm around my shoulder, she whispered softly, "I'm sorry I called you an idiot. I wanted to tell you a *secret*, but I forgot that you're a boy."

"I don't want your secrets," I said. "I've got plenty of my own at home."

She started to laugh, but then ran off, happy that we were more or less friends again.

This time I was coming to Grandfather's bursting with scary news. I felt like a sort of hero coming home from a magic kingdom. I pictured the astonishment I would arouse with what I had to tell. But little did I know that a disturbing surprise was waiting for me in that old house: Margarita.

The moment I stepped through the courtyard gate and looked up I saw her in one of the upper-storey windows. I had never seen such a beautiful woman's face in a house I could only imagine as a repository of aunts, uncles, Arabic letters and food.

She was sitting near the flowerpots, utterly, miraculously alien; as strange and unexpected as a rose that suddenly blooms one morning on a thorny stem.

"Who's that?" I asked Grandma, a bit taken aback.

"Our new tenant," she said. "We rented her the corner room a week ago."

Margarita smiled through the flowerpots and asked, "Is this your grandson?"

"Yes," Grandma answered.

I felt my ears turn red and ran out through the courtyard gate. As I stood at the gate, I heard something, a flutter of wings. Suzana, I thought.

"So, you've come back," she said.

I had suddenly lost the urge to tell stories about the neighbourhood. "What can I tell you? There's nothing to tell," I said.

"Nothing?" she asked, with disappointment.

"Well, there are some stories about magic."

"Magic? How come? Tell me."

"There are different kinds."

"You don't want to talk about it?"

I remained silent.

"Why don't you want to tell me about it? Go on! Or else tell me about the Italians."

I still didn't say anything.

"You're really stupid," she said. "*Extra-ordi-narily.*"

"Really, *extra-ordi-narily?*"

I took the round lens from my pocket and stuck it to one eye, holding it in place between my cheek and brow. To hold the lens that way I had to distort my whole face and keep my neck frozen stiff. Suzana hated seeing me like that.

"Boo! Monster!" she said.

"I *like* my look."

"Why do you want to look so ugly?"

"Because I feel like it."

I began to move slowly, holding my neck stiff and my face screwed up, tightening every muscle to keep the lens from falling. She looked at me scornfully. For a moment, I forgot my inexplicable irritation with her and, wanting to show off, walked into the gypsies' room with the lens over one eye, provoking the little cries of surprise and wonder that this trick usually aroused in them. On my way out, I felt my cheek going numb. I couldn't hold the lens in place any more, so I took it off and put it back in my pocket.

Suzana saw me take it off and came up to me and said softly, "Why are you always in a bad mood when you come over from your place?"

I looked at her and realised from her expression that she was closer to affection than to resentment. She took a step towards me.

"If you only knew! I'm so alone here. So bored."

Her smile anticipated the kind words I would say, but just then, as if driven by some blind and irresistible force, suddenly and unthinkingly, I blurted out in a drawl that even I didn't recognise as my own the words I had heard an Italian say:

"*Che puttana!*"

She clapped her hands to her mouth, took a step back, then another, then turned and ran away as fast as she could through the undergrowth. I stood there a moment, rooted to the ground. My forehead was covered with sweat. I was brought back to my senses by Grandma calling me for lunch.

I didn't see Suzana again for the four days of my visit. Sometimes I thought I heard a rustle somewhere around me, but I couldn't tell exactly where, and I never did catch sight of her.

Autumn was closing in, the roses in the yard were fading, and everything was getting more barren by the day, but Grandfather's old house had become brighter. These were the last evenings when the gypsies would play their violins. Grandfather, after reading his big books all afternoon, now smoked his pipe in the courtyard in the half-light, reclining on the divan. I would sit near him on a stool as usual, but I'd lost interest in tobacco and Turkish books, for Margarita often sat near me and put her arm around my shoulder. The sky was pitch black, and now and then a falling star flashed in the void.

"A shooting star," Margarita said softly. "Did you see it?"

I nodded.

To tell the truth, a star falling from the sky made about as much impression on me as a button falling off a coat, for Margarita's thick hair was spread across my neck and her hair, her whole body, had a subtle fragrance I had never noticed on Mamma, Grandma or any of my aunts. Nor was it like any of the other smells I liked best, including the aroma of my favourite dishes.

It had grown cooler, and Grandpa got up from the chaise longue earlier now than on summer evenings. Everyone else got up after he did, the gypsies would put their violins back in their cases, and for a moment there would be silence. Then there would be a flash of lightning in the distance, and Grandfather would say, "It's going to rain tomorrow."

"Good night," the Gypsies would say on their way back to their shack.

"Good night," Margarita's husband would say, on the rare occasions he stayed there.

"Good night," Margarita would reply in her warm voice.

"Good night," they would all answer in turn.

I would say "Good night" too, last of all, sleepy as I was. Then the old steps would creak for a while until calm and sleep settled over everything.

Then the ceilings of the house came to life. The movements of mice, timid and sporadic at first, became bolder and more rapid until an unchained horde thundered from one corner of the attic to another. As the minutes passed, my mind turned the mice into the hordes of Genghis Khan, which I had seen in a film. Now they were gathering somewhere in the depths of Asia (Asia was Margarita's ceiling). Getting ready for battle. A brief silence. Genghis Khan must be addressing his troops. He extends his hand toward the borders of Europe (the hall ceiling). The hordes move off. The commotion mounts, the ceilings groan. They cross the frontiers of our continent. The noise builds to a crescendo. Right above our heads. Terror. Carnage. Then the horde veers off. A messenger brings the news from the depths of Asia. A tribe has rebelled. The horde rushes back whence it came. Crosses the border again. Now they are back in Asia. A terrible slaughter begins. Margarita lies sleeping beneath the battlefield. Genghis Khan ought to end the hostilities. Doesn't he realise Margarita is sleeping? But he's not interested. In war there is no sleep, he shouts. And the battle rages on.

In the morning Grandma put her hand on my forehead.

"You talked in your sleep last night," she said. "You don't have a fever, do you?"

"No."

It was my fourth and last day at Grandfather's. After breakfast, I said good-bye and left.

On my way home, carrying a big piece of meat pie and Margarita's name (the pie had been carefully wrapped in paper by Grandma; I'm not sure where I held Margarita's name), I saw some school kids going up Varosh Street. They looked terribly upset. Their teacher Qani Kekezi must have dissected another cat in the classroom.

Nothing had changed at home or in the neighbourhood, but something was going on out on the plain across the river. The first thing I noticed was that the cattle that usually grazed there were gone. The haystacks were being taken away, too. Trucks crisscrossed the plain. Eventually I began to see more clearly what was happening. A new, completely unknown word was cropping up here and there, made up of two other words: "air" and "drome" (we knew that "drome" meant "road" in Greek). Now everything was clear: across the river, in the plain at the foot of the city, an aerodrome was under construction.

Passers-by often stopped in the streets and alleys, turned towards the river, and gazed pensively into the distance.

A new guest had arrived. An unusual guest, lying flat at the city's door, almost invisible. If it weren't for the absence of the cows and haystacks, you might not have even noticed it was there. For my part, I was sorry the cows had gone. I missed the cows.

"Why is it called 'aerodrome'?"

Javer looked at me thoughtfully with his grey eyes.

"Because it is the place where airplanes fly up into the sky."

A guest. For better or for worse? It had crept in noiselessly. Thousands of astonished eyes observed it without fully realising that it was there. Now, stretched out over the whole length of the plain, incomprehensible and threatening, it perplexed everyone.

"War preparations."

"Maybe. But it could also be to defend the city."

"I don't think so. It's a sign that war is on the way."

"Could be. All the same, a lot of people have got work there."

"The money they earn is a loan from death."

That was an exchange between two people I didn't know.

There was more and more talk of the aerodrome. And it was only when they started calling it "aerodrome" that people realised that until then the plain had had no name. Apparently, it had had to wait for the planes to have its christening.

V

When I got back from Babazoti's, I sensed that the magic spells over our neighbourhood had lost almost all of their force. The workmen had also finished cleaning our cistern. Finally free of the powers of darkness, it was now being filled with fresh water, which gurgled joyfully along the eaves. I leaned over the mouth of the cistern and said, "A-oo." Although filled with new and unknown water, it answered me at once. The same voice, just a little fainter. This meant that all the water in the world, whichever part of the sky it fell from, spoke the same language.

Apart from the fact that the cows no longer grazed in the field across the river, nothing worrisome had happened, except for the sudden disappearance of Kako Pino's cat.

She was just now at her window talking about it with Bido Sherifi's wife, who was leaning out of her own window, her hands covered with flour.

"I tell you, he's the one who took your cat, that cursed teacher won't leave a single one alive. He's the one who took it."

"Of course. Who else? It's the end of the world."

Obviously they were talking about Qani Kekezi.

"That's what education does for you, Kako Pino. More harm than good. I ask you: a cat-thief!"

"Yes, he's gone completely crazy," said Kako Pino. "The poor cats are afraid to set foot outside any more. A topsy-turvy world we live in!"

"But that's not all," said Bido Sherifi's wife. "Wait until he starts coming after people with that knife. Have you ever seen eyes like his? Blood-red they are."

Bido Sherifi's wife shook her hands, raising a cloud of flour that caught the sun and glowed as if it was on fire.

"The end of the world," said Kako Pino. "Can't tell who's worse than the others."

The shutters on both windows closed, ending the conversation. I had nothing to do and sat watching the street. A cat was jumping from roof to roof, then came down and crossed the street. Nazo's son, Maksut, was coming home from the market. He carried another severed head under his arm. Whose head? I couldn't stand it, so I looked away.

I tried to picture Margarita, but was surprised to find that I couldn't recall her face very well. She had come into my thoughts two or three times. Did she realise that I dragged her name with me around the house, banging it on the stone, catching it on nails? Did she feel no pain from all that?

The day before I had talked to Ilir about it.

"At Grandfather's, there's now a beautiful married woman," I told him.

He wasn't impressed and didn't answer. A little later I mentioned Margarita to him again. Again he showed no interest, and only asked me, "Does she have pink cheeks?"

"Yes," I answered, somewhat perplexed. "Pink."

Actually, I didn't remember what colour her cheeks were. The moment Ilir asked about her, Margarita's face suddenly seemed misty. A day passed and the image was even less clear. I was forgetting her.

The third time she came to mind, I mentioned her to Ilir again. He stared at me. This time he's going to say something, I thought, feeling happy about it already.

"You know what?" Ilir said. "Last night I stole my mother's garters to make a slingshot. Do me a favour and hold onto them for a few days. I'm afraid she'll find them."

I stuffed the garters into my pocket.

There was no one in the street. I remembered that Javer had promised to give me a book. I left and went to his place.

Javer was alone, smoking a cigarette and whistling to himself.

"You promised you would give me a book," I said.

"*Si, signor*," he said. "Here are the books. Pick one."

There was a shelf of books on the wall. I walked over and looked at them. I couldn't believe my eyes. I had never seen so many books.

"Look," Javer explained, "this is the name of the author, the one who wrote the book, and this is the title. But I'm afraid none of these books will really interest you."

I took a bunch of books off the shelves, one by one. Most of the titles were meaningless to me.

"I'll take this one," I said. "The author is a man called Jung."

Javer burst out laughing.

"You want to read Jung?"

"Why not? He writes about magic, doesn't he?"

Javer laughed again. I was irritated and turned to leave, but he stopped me.

"Look," he said, "take another one instead. I can barely understand Jung myself. Anyway, he didn't write in Albanian."

I looked through the books again and plunged into reading. Javer kept on smoking and humming. Finally I found one that had on its opening page the words "ghost," "witches," "first murderer" and even "second murderer."

"OK, I'll take this one," I said, without even looking at the title.

"Really? *Macbeth*? It'll be too hard for you."

"I want it."

"Then take it," said Javer. "But don't lose it."

I left almost at a run, went home and pushed the door open. I was amazed to have a book in my hands.

There were all kinds of things in our big house: copper cauldrons, plates of all sizes, bread bins, mortars, iron hooks, beams, steel balls (one was supposed to be a cannonball), barrels, chests with dates painted on them, all sorts of buckets, pitchers, and ewers, a rifle with a butt inlaid with mother-of-pearl, a whole clutter of strange old things including a trough for slaking lime — but not a single book. Apart from a torn and yellowing manual of dream interpretation, there wasn't a single sheet of printed paper in the house.

I closed the door and scurried upstairs at top speed. There was no one in the living room. I sat by the window, opened the book, and started to read. I read very slowly, and hardly understood anything. I read up to a certain point, then started over again from the beginning. Little by little, I began to understand what I was reading. My head was spinning. Outside it was getting dark. The letters started dancing around, trying to jump out of line. My eyes hurt.

After dinner, I went to the kerosene lamp and opened the book again. The letters looked frightening in the yellow lamplight.

"That's enough reading," my mother decreed. "Go to bed."

"You sleep, I'm going to read."

"No," she said. "We don't have enough kerosene."

I couldn't get to sleep. The book lay nearby. Silent. A thin object on the divan. It was so strange . . . Between two cardboard covers were noises, doors, howls, horses, people. All side by side, pressed tightly against one another. Decomposed into little black marks. Hair, eyes, legs and hands, voices, nails, beards, knocks on doors, walls, blood, the sound of horseshoes, shouts. All docile, blindly obedient to the little black marks. The letters run in mad haste, now here, now there. The *h*'s, *r*'s, *o*'s, *t*'s gallop over the page. They gather together to create a horse or a hailstorm. Then gallop away again. Now they create a dagger, a night, a ghost. Then streets, slamming doors, silence. Running and running. Never stopping. Without end.

I slept so fitfully I thought I had a fever. Through the sleep I could just barely feel a steady laboured breathing coming from outside, a painful shifting of streets and neighbourhoods. The city seemed to be scratching itself in slow motion. It was a pain of transformation. The streets swelled, twisted. The walls of houses grew thick and turned into the battlements of Scottish castles. Fearsome keeps loomed up here and there.

In the morning, the city looked worn out from its trials. It had changed. But not that much.

I spent almost all day reading.

Night fell again. I looked outside at the walls and buildings. My mind was on fire. All the normal limits on the shape of things seemed to have been suspended. They could turn into anything now.

Aqif Kashahu was trudging down Varosh Street with his two boys. He turned into our street. Kako Pino stuck her head out of the window, then went back inside. Bido Sherifi's great double gate was open. Aqif Kashahu was going towards it. It was obvious: this must be his last night. Bido Sherifi himself came to the gate to greet his distinguished guest. Bido's wife leaned out of her window for a moment, then disappeared. Kako Pino did the same. The signs were clear. Aqif Kashahu and his heirs went inside. The great gates swung shut with a metallic clatter. *Flourish.*

"Why do you stay shut up in the house all day? Go out and play with your friends."

"Ssh, Grandmother."

I was waiting to hear Aqif Kashahu's death scream. It must have all been over by now. I heard a knock. Then another. Bido Sherifi's wife appeared in the window. She was trying to wash the blood from her hands. She shook them. A cloud of flour drifted down. The flour was red with blood.

Grandmother put her hand on my forehead.

Another flourish of trumpets came from downstairs.

"Go and see the big cauldron they're taking out of the basement," said Grandmother. "I don't have the heart to watch."

For several days, they had been talking about selling the big copper cauldron. Now the dealer had come, and the big cauldron, as it left the house, was chiming farewell. *Trumpets and alarum within.*

Night had fallen. Again the city sank into a darkness peopled with keeps, foreign names and owls.

"That book has addled your brain," Grandmother said. "Go to Grandfather's tomorrow to clear your mind."

"All right, I'll go."

Margarita . . .

I was exhausted. My head sank onto the windowsill.

The next day I set out for Grandfather's. When I passed the Bridge of Brawls and turned into Citadel Street the city was suddenly freed of its keeps and night-owls. I was almost running for the last part of the way.

"Where's Margarita?" I asked Grandma, who was kneading dough for bread rolls.

"What do you want with Margarita?" she asked. "You'd do better to start by asking how Grandfather is, or your aunts and uncles, instead of starting right out with 'Where's Margarita?'"

"She's not gone, is she?"

"No, she's still here," Grandma said in a mocking tone, muttering to herself as she kept on kneading dough.

I wandered around the house for a while and then, since I had nothing else to do, I went up to the roof where I liked to sit for hours on the light-coloured, slanting slates near the old dormer. People looked different from the roof. I was watching a half-rotten telegraph pole when I remembered the box I had filled with Grandfather's cigarette butts and had hidden in the attic, along with a Turkish book and a box with two or three matches. I really wanted to smoke on the roof, holding in my lap the Turkish book with its sickly, yellowing pages.

I was thinking about lighting a cigarette, so I crawled to the dormer, stuck my arm through the pieces of dusty broken glass, and took out the book first, then the box of tobacco, and finally the matchbox. The cover of the book was mouldy and the pages, which had got wet, were stuck together. I tore off a piece of the back cover and though the tobacco looked a little mouldy too, I rolled a cigarette as well as I could, took it in my mouth and tried to light it. But the match was wet and wouldn't light.

I put everything back on a blackened beam in the attic, and as I was shaking the dust off my arm, I got another idea.

The old attic was just above Margarita's room. Once it had provided light for the small hallway, but when part of the hallway was turned into a room, the attic became useless; it didn't light anything any more.

The idea that I could see what Margarita was doing shook me out of my lethargy. To be safe, I pulled out the fragments of broken glass still hanging in the window frame, then put one foot through and onto a beam and slipped in under the roof. I started climbing downwards, clinging to the blackened beams that crisscrossed in every direction. A minute later I was on the ceiling of her room. I moved slowly and noiselessly, crawling on my stomach until I came to a crack. I peered through.

The room was empty.

Where could Margarita be? On the blanket she used as

a bedspread some pieces of delicate underwear were neatly folded. I heard a splash and realised that she was taking a bath.

I waited a long time for her to come out of the bath. She was all wrapped up in a big bathrobe, her hair hanging down loose, still wet. She went to the mirror, picked up a comb, and started to run it through her hair. She sang softly to herself:

> In far-away Holland
> In the land of windmills . . .

Still singing, she took her powder-box from the dressing table and undid her bathrobe. Puffy clouds wafted from her cleavage and her armpits as if she was an extraterrestrial being.

When she took off her robe entirely and leaned over to take her underwear from the bed, I closed my eyes. When I opened them, the lace on her body was like white butterflies perched in arcs across her breasts, hips and the tops of her thighs, like those white butterflies of the fields that come out in the spring and that I had chased so often without ever catching one.

I was lying there in a daze, when I heard Grandma's voice. She was looking all over for me. My aunt was calling too, from the courtyard.

I got up carefully and climbed back over the beams, hoisted myself onto the roof again and slid down along the back wall of the house.

"Where were you?" asked Grandma. "How did you get so filthy?"

"On the roof," I answered.

"What were you doing on the roof? You'll shift the slates and when it rains we'll have leaks again."

"No, Grandma, I was careful."

"I doubt it," she said. "Come on, it's time to eat."

Grandma always smelled like fresh bread, and whenever I got hungry, I always thought of her, with her milky complexion and her spreading shape which set the old joists of our house groaning, as if to protest: "Ouch! Grandma, you're crushing us, and we can't take any more."

Grandfather said those ritual Turkish words that always seemed magical to me, and we all started eating. I noticed that Grandma seemed angry because the pans and spoons in her hands were more than usually noisy. Whenever she was angry her gestures were rougher. Finally she couldn't contain herself any more and burst out, "The hussy!"

The word made no impression on the others, who calmly went on chewing. They all seemed to know who she was talking about.

"Who's a hussy, Grandma?" I asked.

Grandfather shot her a disapproving look, and she nodded her head, still looking furious, as if to say, "Yes, all right, all right."

"None of your business," she said to me, suddenly taking the pot from the table.

"If it had been me," said the older of my aunts, "I would've grabbed it right out of her hands."

"What next! I wouldn't stoop to fight with such trash."

I could never imagine Grandma fighting with anyone; all my life I had never seen her doing anything but cooking and kneading dough for her bread.

"Drop the subject," Grandfather said, tilting his head in my direction. Everyone obeyed, but Grandma still seemed angry, for the pans were being banged around even louder. Grandfather, who couldn't stand noise, was the first to leave the table.

"Dirty hussy," Grandma started up again.

"You should've grabbed it right off the clothesline yourself," my elder aunt said again.

My younger aunt opened the newspaper and started reading.

"Put the paper down," said Grandma. "Papers are for men."

My aunt burst out laughing.

"What's so funny? You see everyone's upset and all you can do is sit there reading the paper and laugh."

My aunt got up and walked out, taking the newspaper with her.

"Today the table linen, tomorrow the spoons, and next the carpets," Grandma went on.

Now they were talking about it openly and I realised what was happening. Margarita was stealing.

"Why have you left your food on your plate?" my other aunt asked.

"I'm full," I said, getting up from the table.

"You hardly ate a thing. You're not sick, are you?"

"No."

"Of course you are," said Grandma. "You've caught your death. Sitting on the roof all day as if you had no home."

I got up without a word and went into the living room.

My younger aunt was sitting in the corner reading the news-paper.

I didn't speak to her. The room was completely quiet. From the top of Citadel Street came the song of the stranger as he made his way down:

> *The clock struck seven as I came by;*
> *I stood by your window and sighed a sigh*

I listened, in a dream . . . So, towards seven in the evening, someone else was now going past the windows of a house where a girl called Miriam still lived, and who still had headaches.

The voice faded into the distance but before it disap-peared altogether the wind brought me an extra part of the story:

> *Gladly would I fetch the doctor for you*
> *But neighbours would likely take a dim view*

But why would the neighbours object? What harm would it do to them? I couldn't imagine. I wracked my brains to no end, but then I took comfort in recalling that one day, in the great living room, I'd heard it said that what happens in songs isn't at all like what happens in life.

You could feel autumn coming on. Down below, among the branches losing their leaves, slid a shadow. Suzana. She must have known that I had come.

The tick-tock of the big clock was making a strange

sound. Sadness was all around, spreading in great concentric circles through endless space. Soon it would spread out over the whole world.

It was a gloomy lunch. We ate in silence. Everyone seemed to be waiting impatiently for Grandmother to look at the cock's bones.

In these past days, whenever a rooster was killed in the neighbourhood, everyone was informed right away, because the future could be read in the bones and everyone was expecting something serious to happen.

A week before, Ilir's mother had sent us all over to Kako Pino's. "She slaughtered a cock today," Ilir's mother had said. "Go on over there, children, and find out how the bones came out."

We too had slaughtered a cock today. By afternoon people would be knocking at the door to ask about the bones. Grandmother would be asked about them if she went anywhere; my mother would be questioned the moment she stepped out through the gate, and Papa probably at the coffee house. It should be obvious from all this that in our city people did not get to eat chicken very often.

Lunch came to an end. Grandmother picked up the carcass, squinted, and stared hard at it, turning it this way and that, holding one side and then the other up to the light. We all waited in silence.

"War," Grandmother said suddenly in a muffled voice. "The edges of the carina are red. War and blood." She pointed to the places on the breastbone that foretold war.

No one spoke.

Grandmother kept looking at the bone.

"War," she repeated, putting her left hand on my head as if to protect me from some scourge.

After lunch, I went back to the pile of dirty dishes to look for the bone. I took it up the two flights to the main room, where I sat alone at the high windows and began a careful examination of that tragic bone. It was an October afternoon. A dry wind was blowing. I stared at the cold bone I held in my hand. It was reddish, shading into violet. Sometimes it seemed splattered with little drops of blood, sometimes it blazed with the reflections of a great fire.

Gradually it turned completely red, its back now covered no longer with little drops of blood but with whole streams rushing down the slopes, turning everything in their path red.

As I fell asleep with the bone in my hand, I saw the flames blazing on its side once more. Then, as if through a wall of smoke, I heard the first drums of war.

I could feel it the moment I entered the courtyard: Margarita was gone. I didn't ask what had happened. The street was deserted, and the courtyard trees were losing their leaves, which fluttered lazily onto the roof of the shack where the gypsies lived. I felt sad.

The autumn rains would start soon. The trees would be completely bare, and the wind would howl through the eaves. The roof would leak in the places I had sat in the summer, and in the old attic, the box of tobacco, the matches and the Turkish book would rot away.

Suzana would flutter about in the air somewhere and never find out what had happened to a man called Macbeth in distant Scotland. I wouldn't have been surprised if, the next time I came, they had told me that she'd flown off with the storks.

On winter nights, the hordes of mice would rage up and down in the attic. Fight on, Genghis Khan. Crush everything in your path. No one sleeps below Asia any more. It's just a desert.

FRAGMENT OF A CHRONICLE

his declaration. During the Polish campaign I never ordered a night-time air raid, Adolf Hitler claims. I bombed the country by day. I did the same in Norway, Belgium and France. Then suddenly Mr Churchill bombed Germany at night. You know how patient I am, Comrades. I waited a week. He bombed again. This man is mad, I said to myself. I waited two weeks. Many people came to me and said, "Führer, how much longer do we have to stand for this?" Then I gave the order to bomb England by night. Trial. Executive measures. Property. One hundred and twenty-seventh session. Angoni vs Karllashi. The chronicler Xivo Gavo refused to assist in clarifying the matter of the old land titles. Our fellow citizen the inventor Dino Çiço is preparing to leave on a trip to Hamburg. We take the opportunity to protest indignantly at an article in a Tirana newspaper headlined "World War Imminent. Mad Inventor Claims Creation of Device to Protect Town." Yesterday our fellow citizen T.V. drank thirty cups of coffee in a row. I order a blackout in the city. Garrison Commander Bruno Arcivocale. Na-

VI

I was coming home from Grandfather's. I had stayed longer than usual because this was to be my last visit of the year. In the winter hardly anyone went to see him because the weather was too bad and the place was battered by the wind from all directions. Only my father would sometimes venture out into that wasteland to borrow a little money.

As soon as I came into the house, I could tell that something had changed. Mamma and Grandmother were darning an old blanket. Nazo's daughter-in-law was helping.

"What are you doing?" I asked.

"We have to cover the windows at night," Grandmother said. "Government orders."

"What for?"

"In case of bombing. Didn't they tell you about it over there?"

I shrugged.

"No, I don't know anything about it."

"They went from house to house announcing it," Grandmother said.

Someone knocked furiously at the door.

"Xhexho," Mamma said.

It was indeed Aunt Xhexho, and she was already halfway up the stairs.

"How are you, ladies?" she said, out of breath from her climb. "Sewing curtains? God, what a disaster. What next? To have to cover the house like a tomb. Harilla Lluka has been going from door to door since this morning. 'Darkness,' he says, 'Let there be darkness.'"

"Compulsory blackout," said Nazo's daughter-in-law without raising her eyes from the blanket. "That's what it's called."

"May they be struck blind!" Xhexho exclaimed. "May their eyes go as dim as Vehip Qorri's!"

I didn't understand who Xhexho was cursing or why.

There was another knock at the door. It was Kako Pino and Nazo.

"Have you heard?" asked Kako Pino. "They say we have to block up the chimneys too. The end of the world!"

"Let them close up everything!" shouted Xhexho. "The chimneys and doors, and even the toilets if they want. The world's gone mad, my good Pino, mad. Everything's going to the dogs."

"It's crazy, all right," Kako Pino agreed. "Barely one wedding a week. The end of the world!"

"They chase the cows out of the field and cover it with cement. Have you ever seen anything like it, Selfixhe? They say there's a man called Yusuf, a man with a red beard, Yusuf Stalin his name is, who's going to smash them all to pieces."

"Is he a Muslim?" Nazo asked.

Xhexho hesitated a moment, then said confidently, "Yes. A Muslim."

"That's a good start," said Nazo.

They all started talking, Nazo speaking to Grandmother while Xhexho whispered in Maksut's wife's ear, as if to ask her something. She shook her head without looking up from the blanket. Xhexho put her hands to her cheeks in despair.

The conversation got more intense. Now they were speaking in pairs, in low and level tones, except for Kako Pino and Nazo's daughter-in-law.

"Well, that really is the end of the world," Kako Pino suddenly said, not to anyone in particular. Then she got up and left. Nazo and her daughter-in-law followed.

The whole neighbourhood was worried, that was clear. The way shutters opened and closed, the knocks at doors here and there, the constant howl of the dry wind, and even the way the women hung out the sheets — all seemed to pass on the general anxiety.

People couldn't get used to the draped windows. Some found it ridiculous, most said it was absurd, and still others considered it an ill omen. On the third night, Bido Sherifi took down a curtain, but just a few minutes later a harsh, angry voice came up from the street:

"*Spegni la luce!*"

Two nights later, when the machine-gun at the lookout post fired on the house of the chronicler Xivo Gavo, whose lamp was the last in the city to be extinguished, everyone realised that the *oscuramento* was no joke. Night after night, an angry eye kept watch, checking every point and all directions. No light ever escaped his attention.

So the city submitted tamely to the blackout. As night fell, the town gradually blurred; streets and roofs wobbled as if suffering vertigo, minarets and chimneys tottered as if suspended in mid-air, then disappeared with everything else. *Oscuramento*.

The construction project was another topic of daily conversation. The word "aerodrome" was mangled without mercy by the gums and stumps of all the city's old women and came out so distorted as to be virtually unrecognisable. Yet these *r*'s, *d*'s and *m*'s (grains of sand watered with saliva), even when kneaded together in such comical ways, retained an extraordinary capacity to spread fear.

They were working day and night in the plain, which everyone now called "aerodrome plain." Thousands of soldiers and hundreds of trucks rolled back and forth all day, doing something that from afar looked like nothing at all. From time to time the noise of the stone-crushers, cement mixers and polishing machines drifted up into the city.

About that time there were a number of robberies in the city. Taking advantage of the blackout, thieves were lifting off slates and getting into houses from the roofs. (Most burglaries in the city had always been done from the roofs.)

Not long after the first break-ins, an unknown aircraft flew over the city. It was so high up that no one would have noticed it had it not been for the unfamiliar, low throbbing noise it made, which came in waves, like an unending roll of thunder. It left a kind of stupefaction in its wake, drifting above us, hanging in the white clouds.

In the days that followed, other planes passed overhead, too, almost always alone and so high that they seemed intent on showing that they had nothing to do with our city. Whose were they? Where did they come from? Where were they going? What for? The sky was as impenetrable as it was indifferent.

The rooftop break-ins might well have got worse except for the appearance of a new monster: the searchlight. It had crept into the city in complete silence without anyone even suspecting its existence until suddenly, one October night, its one eye, like the eye of a Cyclops, lit up the stony river bed. A long arm of light stretched out like a transparent reptile seeking the city. It seemed pallid in the pit of darkness, but, when it hit the first roofs, the cone of light brightened and, with cruel clarity, began gliding over the fronts of the houses, which turned white with terror.

The same thing happened on subsequent nights. Every night the searchlight sought out the city in the dark and once it had found it, clutched onto it. Its beam was a jelly-like sea-creature that slithered over neighbourhoods, constantly changing its shape to fit the contours of the streets and houses on which it fell.

Around that time, the visits of the aged *katenxhikas* became predictably more frequent. Unlike the old crones, the *katenxhikas* were old ladies who often left their houses, especially in times of trouble. They were different in other ways as well. They still complained about their daughters-in-law, for example, whereas the daughters-in-law of the old crones had long since left this world. The *katenxhikas* also complained of rheumatism, gout and various other illnesses, whereas the old crones suffered only the noble disability of blindness, about which they never complained. In short, the *katenxhikas* were nothing like the crones.

As usually happened after strange events, the *katenxhikas*

poured through the streets and alleyways. In Citadel Street and Old Market Street, Upper and Lower Palorto, in the town square and on the Bridge of Brawls, in Dashu Square, in the gallery of the Christian Pasha, below the Citadel, over the Owls' Valley, on Chain Square, in alleys with no name, they walked and walked in the sparse rain, wrapped in their black shawls, going down Varosh Street and back up Dunavat, hunched up, out of breath, and full of gossip.

A cold, dry wind blew steadily down from the mountain passes to the north. I listened to its uniform howl, and for some reason the expression "words are gone with the wind" went round and round in my head. Something strange was happening to me lately. Everyday words or expressions, things I had heard dozens of times, were suddenly taking on new meanings in my mind. The words were casting off their usual idiomatic sense. Expressions made up of two or three words would painfully fall apart. If I heard someone say, "My head is boiling," despite myself I couldn't help imagining a head boiling like a pot of beans. Words had a certain force in their normal state. But now, as they began to shear and crack up, they acquired amazing energy. I was afraid they would explode. I did all I could to stop it, but in vain. Chaos reigned in my head as words, devoid of logic and reality, abandoned themselves to their *danse macabre*. Common oaths like "You can eat your own head!" tormented me most of all. The horrific vision of someone holding his head in his hands and devouring it was compounded by the trouble I had understanding how anyone could eat his own head when everyone knows that you eat with your teeth and teeth are in the head, whether it be cursed or not.

Ordinary speech, once serene and reassuring, had been shaken as by an earthquake. Everything was upside down, falling apart, breaking up.

I had entered the kingdom of words, where a merciless tyranny reigned. The world was suddenly filled with people who had pumpkins for heads. Others had heads that spun and eyes that threw knives. Some had blood that froze like ice, others wandered about with forked tongues, gold fingers or iron fists. A slab of flesh pierced by two eyes would pop up here or there. The city itself was feverish (I had seen the window panes shiver, and had even seen their greyish sweat). Someone was walking around on his unearthed roots. Others, like madmen, asked idiotic questions: "Where are your ears? Where are your eyes?" Someone was trying to devour someone else not with his teeth but with his eyes. Unknown painters were blackening the door of a house or the fate of some young girl (where did these painters come from, I wondered, and why were they doing this, and anyway why did people care so much whether their destiny was painted black or white?). And, one fine day, a young man was smitten by love's arrow. The world was falling apart before my very eyes. Surely that was what Kako Pino meant when she said, as she never stopped saying, "It's the end of the world."

It was one of those days when the power of words was at its peak. I was scouring the sloped roofs to see if I could find out where love had hidden before smiting a young man with its arrow. But unlike even small stones thrown down from that height, love didn't make you bleed or leave a bump on your head. Why, then, in spite of that, did people complain about it so much, especially when it landed on a girl?

I was rescued from these thoughts by a knocking at the door that echoed through the whole house. We all recognised Xhexho's knock. But the way she knocked this time, and the short spaces between blows, told us that something unusual had happened. With a worried look on her face, Mamma went down to open the door, while Grandmother stood waiting at the top of the stairs.

Then she too went down. The upper floors fell silent. The door opened. Someone came in. Someone else went out. Then someone came in again. The muffled sounds of women's voices reached my ears. I tiptoed down the steps, trying not to attract attention. There was definitely something serious going on downstairs. The door creaked again. A hum of words I could not clearly distinguish filled the air like a haze. No one noticed me. They were standing by the railing next to the cistern, at the foot of the stairs. Besides Xhexho there was Nazo and her daughter-in-law, as well as Kako Pino, Bido Sherifi's wife, and another neighbour. The frantic look in their eyes, the way Xhexho's scarf had slid back to reveal a tuft of greyish hair, and the marks on their cheeks from recent gestures of indignation all told me that something irreparable had occurred. They were all talking at once. Something monstrous had indeed happened, but I couldn't figure out what was. It wasn't death or madness. Something worse. Xhexho stood in the centre of them all, and her grating wheeze, like a black-smith's bellows, fanned their fear.

I listened for a long time, but I still couldn't understand what it was all about. They were talking about some kind of house. The Italians had opened a business of some kind. It was called something that sounded quite easy. It was a word that had the sound "board" in it, like "boarding house." Yet they were terrified. They cursed it. I had heard about a sugar house where beautiful young girls lived. This one must have been made of poison to throw the whole city into such turmoil.

"One man from every house," Xhexho said, her voice low and strange. "That's what they said. And if they don't go of their own accord, they'll be dragged there by brute force. One male from every family."

The women pinched their cheeks again. Only Nazo's daughter-in-law seemed unmoved. Xhexho cast her eyes about. They fell on me.

"Don't you get any ideas about going there!" she exclaimed.

"Idiot," said Grandmother. "Leave the boy alone."

"The end of the world," said Kako Pino, for at least the hundredth time

"Will our folk ever come to their senses?" Xhexho cried, addressing Grandmother as if she were the representative of the city.

Just then there was another knock at the door. It was Aunt Xhemo.

"What's the matter, poor things? Why are you so upset?" she asked, the moment she set foot in the hallway.

Aunt Xhemo didn't come to visit us very often, maybe two or three times a year. She was tall and straight and seemed to be all skin and bone. In the family she was known for her mania for cleanliness. She would never eat anything that had been touched by someone else. Bread, all her meals, coffee, tea — she prepared everything with her own hands. At home, she kept her own spoon, plate, cup and coffee pot separate.

If she went visiting, she would bring along her own bread wrapped in a clean cloth, and her coffee pot, cup, spoon and glass wrapped in another. Everyone understood her mania, and no one was offended when she sat down at the table and unwrapped her simple fare.

Aunt Xhemo listened in silence as the other women discussed the strange new establishment.

"You're crazy to go on like this," she finally said. "I was wondering what was happening. I thought they were opening this . . . this what do you call it, this communal canteen."

Aunt Xhemo had always been worried about the existence of canteens. In her mind it was the worst possible calamity.

"Why are you fretting over a bordello?" she cried. "I could understand someone with a young husband being concerned," she said, glancing at Nazo's daughter-in-law. "But why should you care? Don't be so silly!"

Nazo's daughter-in-law smiled and, to everyone's astonishment, put her hand to her mouth, and burst out laughing. Nazo nudged her in the ribs with her elbow.

The gathering adjourned. Grandmother and Aunt Xhemo slowly climbed back up the two flights of wooden stairs.

"Whatever will we hear about next, Selfixhe?" Aunt Xhemo sighed.

"When foreigners set foot in the country, you have to be ready for anything," Grandmother answered. "A young girl can't sit in the window any more without the Italians taking out pocket mirrors and flashing signals at her."

"It was obvious from the day they arrived that they were

fops," said Aunt Xhemo. "God knows I've seen my share of armies, but I never thought I'd come across soldiers wearing perfume."

"If that were all, I wouldn't mind. But what I don't like is what they're doing down there," said Grandmother, nodding towards the airfield.

Aunt Xhemo sighed. "War is at our doorstep, Selfixhe."

Meanwhile, the women at their windows kept talking about the new business in the house they called a "board." All the lightning in the heavens was called down upon it. A hundred times a day it was consumed by flames, reduced to ashes, but it must have arisen from those ashes every time, for the curses continued to rain down.

A new wave of *katenxhikas* flooded the streets and alleys. The cold wind still blew from the northern mountain passes, fluttering the black scarves of the *katenxhikas* and making their eyes water with teardrops that filled out like glass beads. They walked up and down, never stopping.

The city was truly sick. Now it was easy to see it sweating. Windows often shivered convulsively. Chimneys groaned. Every night the searchlight's one eye lit up. Polyphemus. I dreamed of creeping up on it with a red-hot poker to put out that horrible eye. And I imagined the blinded searchlight would scream with pain all night long.

They were troubled times, and everything was uncertain. I thought of the shifting landscape around Grandfather's house. It looked as if the ground around our house would soon start moving too. Everyone thought so.

Ilir raced down Fools' Alley.

"Guess what?" he said, as he came through the door.

"The world is round like a melon. I saw it at home. Isa brought it. It's round, perfectly round, and it spins without stopping."

He took a long time to tell me just what he had seen.

"But how come they don't fall off?" I asked when he told me there were other cities under us, full of people and houses.

"I don't know," Ilir said. "I forgot to ask Isa. He and Javer were home looking at the globe. Then Javer tapped it with his finger and said, 'Soon it'll be a slaughterhouse.'"

"A slaughterhouse?"

"Yes. That's what he said. The world will drown in blood. That's what he said."

"Where will all the blood come from?" I asked. "Fields and mountains don't have blood."

"Maybe they do," said Ilir. "They must know something, the way they talk. When Javer said the world would be a slaughterhouse, I told him we'd been there and had seen how they slaughter sheep. He started laughing and said, 'Now you'll see what happens when they slaughter nations.'"

"Nations? Like on the postage stamps, you mean?"

"Right. Like that. Nations."

"Who's going to slaughter them?"

Ilir shrugged. "I didn't ask."

I thought about the slaughterhouse again. One day when she was talking about the aerodrome Xhexho said that the fields and grasses would be covered with cement. With wet slippery cement. A rubber hose sluicing cities and nations. To wash away the blood . . . Maybe we were only at the beginning of the slaughter. But I found it hard to imagine nations being led to the slaughter, bleating as they went. Peasants in their black woollen cloaks. Butchers in white coats. Rams, ewes, lambs. People standing around to watch. Other people just waiting. Then it was time. France. Norway. The square awash with blood. Holland bleating. Luxembourg like a newborn lamb. Russia with a big bell around its neck. Italy a goat (I don't know why). Something mooing all on its own. Who could that be?

"Well, what do you hear about this house they're all talking about?" Ilir asked.

"I heard it's bad. Very bad."

"You know what? They say it's full of beautiful young girls."

"Really? Xhexho says they're bad women."

"But beautiful."

"Beautiful? You're crazy."

"You're the one who's crazy!"

Both of us shut up for a while.

Meanwhile the bordello had set the whole town abuzz. Xhexho swept in and out of our house several times a day, bringing the most incredible news. The wind blew constantly. There had not been such powerful gusts of wind for decades. They said that old Xivo Gavo had decided to mention the windstorm in his chronicle.

Around that time, they had the first air-raid siren tests. At noon there came a wail that froze the marrow of our bones.

"That must be Bido Sherifi's mother-in-law," Grandmother said. "Nobody else can shriek like that."

Papa and Mamma leaned on the windowsill. The wailing continued, but it was no human cry. It came in waves, seemed to fade away and then suddenly rose again, rending the heavens

93

with yet more power. Not even a hundred of Bido Sherifi's mothers-in-law could have made such a sound.

"It's a siren," my father said bleakly. "I heard one once in Egypt."

Grandmother was dumbfounded.

So it was that the city came to have a siren.

"Now we have a mourner who will wail for us all," said Xhexho, who had come to visit that afternoon. "That's all we needed, Selfixhe. All we have to do now is wait for the archangel to gather up our souls."

As if all this were not enough, something else happened that shook even those who had kept calm until then. Argjir Argjiri was getting married.

I had noticed that announcements of engagements or weddings sometimes surprised people, making some happy and bringing smiles to others. But I never thought the news of a wedding could be seen by everyone, without exception, as a major catastrophe. Have you heard? Argjir Argjiri is getting married. You're kidding! No, really, it's true. Don't talk nonsense. Argjir Argjiri getting married? How? Well, he is. Come on! It's impossible. No it isn't. Kako Pino has even been summoned to paint the bride. No, it's unbelievable. It can't be. But I heard the same thing. It's true then? Yes, it's true. God, what an abomination. How shameful!

Argjir Argjiri was a short dark man with a voice so high-pitched he sounded like a woman. Everyone knew him, he roamed around in all the neighbourhoods. People said he was half-woman and half-man, and he was the only male, or supposed male, who came and went freely in every house even when the men weren't home. Argjir helped the women with various household chores, looked after the children when the women were at the wash-house, went to fetch water with them and retailed gossip. He had a house of his own, and people said that he helped women not because he had to but because he liked their company and women's work. This was after all not so strange, given that Argjir Argjiri was half-man and half-woman. Although for years he had been the butt of jokes and the object of jeers, by way of compensation he had won a right enjoyed by no other man: he could mingle freely with our city's women and girls.

And now suddenly Argjir Argjiri announced that he was getting married. It was a terrible act of defiance.

The creature with the effeminate voice suddenly declared his manhood. For years he had borne the most biting taunts, awaiting his hour of revenge. The city scowled at such an intolerable outrage. There wasn't a single home Argjir Argjiri had not entered, not a single woman he didn't know. Dark suspicion stalked the town.

Hopes that the reports were false soon evaporated. Kako Pino was summoned. An orchestra was hired, the wedding date was set. Hopes that Argjir Argjiri would change his mind likewise dwindled. Even repeated threats, so rumours said, had no effect. He remained adamant. More pressure was put on him, but he stood his ground. It was all done very discreetly, through clenched teeth and in anonymous letters. No one wanted to lead the campaign against Argjir Argjiri openly, for fear of seeming to have a personal axe to grind.

No one ever found out why the man with the treble voice suddenly rebelled. What had happened to him? Why was he doing it? That's right, why? At last the wedding night arrived. The city was under curfew. The wind that had been blowing for two weeks suddenly stopped. The silence seemed deeper after its incessant whistling. The eye of the searchlight blinked, then went out. The wedding drums rolled as if tolling the death of the city's honour.

"The cup runneth over," Xhexho commented bitterly. Now, she said, we could expect the springs to gush black water.

"That's all we needed," Isa said to Javer as he smoked in the dark. "The marriage of that hermaphrodite."

"Things are all adrift," Javer answered. "This town is going to wind up like Sodom and Gomorrah."

The attack was swift and merciless. The siren failed to give a warning in time. The city was gripped by convulsions, like an epileptic. It pitched over, nearly fell. It was a Sunday, nine in the morning. On that October day near mid-century, the ancient city, pounded countless times through the ages by catapult and cannon, shell and battering ram, was attacked from the sky for the first time. Broken foundations groaned with pain like blinded men. Thousands of terrified windows spewed their shattered panes.

After the infernal thundering, the world went deaf and dumb. The distraught city gazed up at a clear sky, which seemed to beg forgiveness for having stood by and watched. The three tiny silver crosses that had shaken that immense mass of stone to its foundations were now moving off into the distance.

The bombing left sixty-two dead. Granny Neslihan was found in the rubble, buried up to her waist. She didn't understand what had happened to her. Waving her long arms in the air, she cried, "Who killed me?" She was 142 years old. And blind.

FRAGMENT OF A CHRONICLE

Prepare for an air raid. Build yourself a shelter to protect you and yours from the British bombs. Have sandbags ready and store water in the house. Get a hatchet, a shovel and a pickaxe to fight fire. City hall. Trial. Executive measures. Property. Trials are suspended until further notice. Our fellow townsman Argjir Argjiri was found dead in the bridal chamber the morning after his ill-fated marriage. The city could not forgive the man who had so disgraced it. Dr S. Çuberi. Venereal diseases. Daily from four to eight p.m. List of casualties of the latest

VII

The city was bombed every day that week. Everything else was forgotten. No one talked of anything but bombs and planes. Hardly a word was even said about the death of Argjir Argjiri, who was found murdered at dawn, just a few hours after his wedding. His killers, like the authors of the threatening letters, were never identified.

On the seventh day of bombing, something happened that was not without importance. A tin plaque was put up in our street. Some strangers came by early in the morning and nailed it to the wall of our house, to the right of the front door. In big black letters it read: "Air-raid shelter for 90 persons."

There were no other signs in our street. We had never seen anything but a few posters giving city ordinances, and they peeled off in two or three days, soaked by the rain and torn by the wind. Obscene graffiti were occasionally scrawled on the walls of houses in chalk or charcoal. But not often. The first real placard was the one nailed to the right of our door.

That day passers-by stopped in front of it and those who could read explained it to the others.

"Is this house for sale?"

"No, Grandpa. It's about something else."

"What?"

"It says we should come and hide in this cellar when the planes drop their bombs."

"Really?"

I stood at the door smiling at passers-by as if to say, "See, that's what you call a house." I was very proud. There were many large and beautiful houses in our neighbourhood, but none of them, not Çeço Kaili's or Bido Sherifi's or even Mak Karllashi's mansion had a plaque like this one. It meant that ours was the strongest of all.

I kept smiling, but to my disappointment no one seemed to pay any attention to me. Except for Harilla Lluka, who when he caught sight of me took off his hat with the greatest respect and nodded in my direction. They said Harilla Lluka was the biggest coward in the neighbourhood.

But the indifference of the adults didn't bother me much. I stayed there at the door and waited impatiently for Ilir to come by. Only a few days before, we had had a long argument about whose house was stronger. We often used to make bets of that kind with each other. Just before that, we had been fighting about how far the king could throw a stone. I said he could throw a stone as far as Holy Trinity hill, while Ilir was adamant that he couldn't throw it farther than the river-bank. At the very most, as far as the bridge, but certainly no further.

Who knows how long this argument would have gone on if we hadn't acquired a new topic for our squabbles! We fought even harder over the relative strengths of our houses, and could have gone on with that fight for a very long time. We might have insulted each other, or even turned to fists or stones, if those strangers hadn't shown up that fine morning and put up the plaque with those marvellous words: "Air-raid shelter for 90 persons."

Probably out of spite, Ilir never showed up. He must have heard about the plaque and sneaked home through the alley.

I waited a long time, then finally got bored and went in. I went straight downstairs to the cellar and stood looking respectfully at its thick walls, which hadn't been whitewashed in ages.

Until then the cellar had never been an important part of the house. We used it to store coal or to slake lime. Compared to the main room two flights up from the ground, the cellar was a kind of scullery maid. This main living room had six big fine windows as tall as my father, and a grainy, mottled ceiling of carved wood. A lot of housekeeping went on in this room. My mother would wash and scrub the floorboards until they shone like wax. The curtains on the windows were white with lace borders, and the room was ringed by low wooden ledges covered with thin mattresses, where old women would sit when they came to visit, sipping their coffee and making sage pronouncements. It was easy to see why the other rooms, even the hallway, were jealous of the main room. Envy could be detected in their constricted windows with their sills out of true and in their hunched, narrow doorways.

But everything changed the day the bombs started falling. The windows in the main room were shattered. The room got upset and lost its looks, while the old cellar, tranquil and kind, cared little about what was going on outside.

I felt sorry for the main room, now abandoned by everyone. During the bombing, while the thick walls of the cellar didn't even vibrate, I felt bad for the main room all alone up there, for I knew it was trembling, shaking all over. I thought of the room as a lady of great beauty now suffering terrible anguish, her nerves strained, while the cellar was an old crone, deaf but tough. As the living room lost its status, the cellar was becoming the most honoured part of the house. It was as if our house had simply been turned upside down.

I would sometimes go up to the living room, now abandoned for good, and look out at the neighbouring houses, their roofs pierced with large holes through which the fine autumn rain now poured. I thought that after the first bombing the same upheaval must have happened in those houses as in ours. Perhaps the damp cellars and basements of the city had been waiting years for this day. Perhaps they had always felt that their time would come.

No doubt about it, these were hard times for the upper floors of the city. When it was built, the wood had cunningly had itself hoisted up top, leaving the stone to the foundations, cellars and cisterns. Down there in the half-darkness, the stone had to fight the rising damp and the groundwater, while the wood, nicely carved and carefully tended, adorned the upper floors. These were light, almost ethereal: the city's dream, its caprice, its flight of fancy. Now the fancy had met its limit. After giving the upper floors such privileges, the city seemed to have changed its mind, and hurried to rectify the error. It had them covered with roofs of slate, as if to establish once and for all that here stone was king.

In any case, I liked this new age of cellar and basement.

All over the city they were putting up metal plaques saying "Air-raid shelter for 15 persons" or "for 22 persons" or "for 35 persons." But plaques saying "Air-raid shelter for 90 persons" were very rare. I was proud of our house. Suddenly it was the centre of the neighbourhood. It had really come to life. We left the gates open so people could come running in at the first sound of the siren. Some even came ahead of time and would sit for hours in the entrance hall leading to the cellar, eating, smoking and chatting.

The cellar was deep underground. A thick wall separated it from the cistern, part of which ran underneath it. A bit of light came in through a narrow slit cut into the foundation slightly above ground level. The air inside was now altogether stuffy.

Our house had become a public place, and not a day passed without some incident. Someone sprained an ankle running down the narrow steps too fast, others argued over room, someone else swore at all the others when they wouldn't let him smoke because it might bother the people who were sick. But most of all they bickered over the best spots. Almost everyone brought along blankets, bedding, and even mattresses, and things got more and more crowded.

"What an age we live in," Bido Sherifi grumbled. "Having to burrow underground like this!"

"These Italian swine will put us through a lot more before they're through," Mane Voco said.

"Not so loud! There may be spies here."

"And the English! Why do they bomb the city instead of dropping their shells on the Italian barracks or the aerodrome?"

"I told you that damned aerodrome would bring the bombs."

"Look, would you lower your voice?"

"Leave me alone," Bido Sherifi replied. "All my life I've lowered my voice."

Besides the usual neighbours, all kinds of other people came. Some I had never seen before, or at least not so close up. Qani Kekezi, squat and ruddy, cast his murky eyes here and there, as if looking for a cat. The women were afraid of him, especially Kako Pino. Lady Majnur, from the rich Kavo family, would go down the cellar stairs holding her nose. Two months earlier I had seen a peasant unloading a mule near the gate of her house. He was so filthy (he and the mule had probably both fallen in the mud) that his face and hands looked as if they were made of earth. From her window Lady Majnur was complaining to a neighbour: "He's the only one who brings the grain he owes me. The other Christian yokels, pardon my language, have started cheating me."

As for Xhexho, there was scarcely any sign of her. That happened from time to time. She would suddenly vanish. But no one worried much about these disappearances, any more than anyone was surprised when she reappeared.

Sometimes our cellar received chance visitors, passersby caught by the bombing or people visiting the neighbourhood. That was how the old artilleryman, Avdo Babaramo, arrived one day with his wife. He sat down near some old men who spent hours airing their views on world affairs in endless conversations in which all kinds of names of states, kings and governments came up. They also talked about Albania a lot. I listened curiously, racking my brain trying to understand exactly what was this Albania they were so worried about. Was it everything I saw around me: courtyards, streets, clouds, words, Xhexho's voice, people's eyes, boredom, or only a part of all that?

"In Smyrna one time," the old artilleryman said, "a dervish asked me, 'Which do you love more, your family or Albania?' Albania, of course, I told him. A family you can make overnight. You walk out of a coffee house, run into a woman on the corner, take her to a hotel, and boom — wife and children. But you can't make Albania overnight after a quick drink in a coffee house, can you? No, not in one night and not in a thousand and one nights either."

"What a way to talk!" his wife said. "You're getting senile. The older you get, the more you blabber on."

"Oh shut up! As if you women knew anything about politics."

"Yes, sir," another old man added. "Albania is a complicated business all right."

"*Ex-treme-ly* complicated. It sure is."

Usually these conversations were interrupted by the siren, and people rushed downstairs. Grandmother always went down last. The stairs creaked in protest at her footsteps. Hurry, Grandmother, hurry! But she never hurried. She always had some reason for being late. Sometimes she was still on the stairs when the first bombs exploded. When she heard the sound, she would make an impatient gesture as if shooing away a fly, and, putting her hands over her ears, she would say, "Go on! Burst away."

I would watch people heading for the stairs, anxious to see Çeço Kaili and his daughter. But the red-headed Çeço never came. He obviously preferred to brave the bombs at home rather than have people see his daughter's beard. Old Xivo Gavo, who spent his days and nights writing his chronicle, didn't come either. The old crones also stayed away. Aqif Kashahu, on the other hand, came with his two sons and his wife and daughter. He was as tall and stout as his daughter was small and frail. She never spoke, just cowered in a corner with a pensive, absent-minded air. Bido Macbeth Sherifi stared at Aqif Kashahu as if he were a ghost. Every time his wife came down into the cellar, she was shaking flour from her hands. And the flour was always red with blood. Aqif Kashahu's ghost looked at everyone in turn. The cellar was full.

"Another air raid!"

The siren was always soft at first, as if awakening from a dream, but then its wailing got more and more raucous. Between two blasts was a valley of silence. A deep valley. Then the peaks of wailing again. Loud and undulating. Pit of silence. Another bout of wailing. Wailing and more wailing. Like trying to use a blanket to smother a piercing shriek that sought only to tear through it. A wild, savage shriek. The whole world is shrieking. Then the bombs. Very near. Then a sudden thunderbolt, an invisible hand turns the world upside down and blows out the two kerosene lamps. Black darkness. A scream rips the darkness. No one moves. We must be dead.

Silence. Then something moves. A noise. Like a match being struck. We are not dead. The match. The pale flame cuts streaks of light in the dark room. Everyone starts moving. All are alive. They light another lamp. But no. Someone is dead. Aqif Kashahu's daughter's thin arms droop lifelessly. Her head too. Her chestnut hair hangs motionless.

At last Aqif Kashahu lets out the scream I had long been expecting. But it's not a cry of pain. A ferocious shriek. The girl's head quivers. She turns round slowly, looking dazed. Her dangling arms contract. The boy in whose arms she was entwined during the bombing also stirs.

"Whore!" Aqif Kashahu screams.

His huge hand grabs her by the hair and he drags her towards the stairs. She tries to get up but falls down again. He hauls her to the middle of the cellar, and only at the foot of the stairs does she somehow manage to get up, scrambling on all fours. He still has hold of her hair.

We could hear the whistling of a dive-bomber outside, but Aqif Kashahu did not turn back. Dragging his daughter by the hair, he went out into the street at the height of the thunderous roar. And so they left under the falling bombs.

The boy had moved back into a corner and was looking at everyone like a trapped animal. I didn't know him. He had light eyes and fair hair. His jaw trembled nervously. Suspiciously, as though expecting someone to jump him any minute, he crossed the cellar through a silence that wasn't silent and went out.

An uproar broke out as soon as he had gone.

"Who in the world was that boy? Where did he come from? Woe betide us!"

"I've never seen him before."

"God, that's all we needed!"

"How shameful!"

"So Kashahu's daughter wasn't as pure as she made out!"

"Deplorable behaviour!"

"She was all over him, like a tart!"

"Like an Italian slut!"

The women pinched their cheeks in despair, adjusted the scarves on their heads, and clucked in indignation. The men stayed stock still.

"Love," Javer muttered through clenched teeth.

Isa watched sadly.

The whole cellar seethed.

The incident was the talk of the town for a long time. People were obsessed by those two arms hanging lifelessly around the neck of a boy whom no one seemed to know. The two thin arms of the girl gradually turned into vicious talons that seized people by the throat, choking off their breath, suffocating them.

But just as from the corpse of one alarming event a new one always sprouts, so the talk about Aqif Kashahu's daughter and her boyfriend was increasingly accompanied by comments about the strange sketches now being made by Dino Çiço, the town inventor.

Dino Çiço had long since given up sleep and was now encroaching on the sleep of others, poring over various calculations and sketches that no one in the region could make head or tail of. The rumour was that these figures had already attracted the interest of some Austrian or Japanese scientists (on this point there were conflicting reports), who had invited him to continue his work in their country, but he had refused. Subsequently Austrian or Portuguese scientists (again their nationality was uncertain) had tried to buy the patent for his invention, but he had declined their offer.

For a long time, our townsman Dino Çiço had worked on his invention in complete secrecy. The exacting task had steadily paled his cheeks and reddened his eyes. The city could recall other men who had devoted their lives to calculations and sketches. Still others preferred direct experimentation. The teacher Qani Kekezi had stated more than once that he learned more from dissecting one cat than from reading any number of anatomy books.

Dino Çiço, however, was completely taken up with his own research. When construction of the aerodrome began at the edge of town, he temporarily laid his regular studies aside and threw himself into work on a new invention. He decided to build an aircraft himself. But this would be a special plane, powered not by an ordinary engine, but by a mechanism based on perpetual motion, or *perpetuum mobile*, as some people called it. Different people pronounced these latter words differently, and the question of pronunciation caused a few arguments, and even exchanges of blows and some broken teeth, which of course further altered the pronunciation of these strange words.

During the first bombing raids, discussion of Dino Çiço's new invention, which would not only assure defence of the city but would also bring honour to its name, became more and more frequent, especially among the old and the very young. Aircraft that run without fuel are the most powerful of all. Fuel-free aircraft are fantastic. They can stay up in the air all day long. My aunt claims they can fly even longer. Can they stay up five days in a row? No, not five days. But why doesn't he build this plane right away? What is he waiting for? Patience, my boy, these things can't be done in a hurry . . .

So we waited.

In the meantime, planes of various kinds, their origin generally unknown, often flew over the city. Every time we raised our eyes to their shining bellies swollen with bombs, we would look automatically towards the dark house with ramshackle eaves, whose owner never ventured out. He was working. Day and night. Go ahead, fly, fly, fly while you can, you pitiful engine-powered planes!

We tried to imagine the chaos Dino Çiço's perpetual-motion plane would wreak in the sky when it first took flight. Black and terrifying, with its strange shape, it would cleave the sky. All the world's planes would flee in terror at the sight of it, tearing off in all directions, some south, some north; others, in total panic, would nose-dive and crash.

But for the moment the city was being bombed regularly every day. Planes circled overhead, quite at ease in the sky. The anti-aircraft battery, which was supposed to have been sent the previous week to defend the city, still hadn't come. After the very first bombing we had all been convinced that besides streets, chimneys and sewers, a city had to have an anti-aircraft battery as well. The old gun, left in the citadel's western tower since the days of the monarchy, had some defect that the municipal mechanics hadn't been able to fix.

The city lay completely defenceless under the autumn sky, which everyone thought looked more open than usual. Never had people craned their necks to peer up into the sky as often as they did that autumn. It was as if they were asking in amazement, "What's the matter with this sky all of a sudden?" For planes were something new in that ancient sky. The thunder, clouds, rain, hail and snow which the sky had always dropped on the city and about which no one was so unreasonable as to complain were nothing compared to this baleful whim of old age. There was something strange and faithless in the heavy masses of cloud and the blue slits that opened suddenly within them like gigantic eyes. The element of treachery was evident even in the monotonous drizzle of rain and the howling wind. More and more, I thought that the world might be better off with no sky at all.

One of those autumn days something happened that I had long been waiting for. It was a Sunday. From the way Grandmother put on her black clothes and shawl, I knew that something unusual was up. She had become almost miraculously agile. I soon realised that she was about to make an extraordinary visit. Open-mouthed, I watched her movements in silence, for fear that one word from me would break the tranquil harmony of the swishing of clothes and hands.

Quivering with excitement, I asked in a near whisper: "Where are you going?"

She stared at me. Her eyes were calm, just a touch far away. She slowly opened her mouth and said: "To Dino Çiço's." I had guessed as much.

"Take me too, please," I begged. She stroked my hair.

"Get dressed," she said.

The cobblestones in the street were wet. It was raining softly. An old song ran through my mind:

> *It's raining, it's pouring*
> *The old lady's snoring . . .*

I had become an old lady, one of the *katenxhikas*. Walking through the rain in my black dress. Going to have coffee. Going to see, going to hear. I was happy.

"Will we see the plane?" I asked.

"We'll see it," she said. "It's right in the middle of the living room."

"But can I see it close up?"

"Close up, yes, but behave yourself. Don't touch anything."

I looked at my hands. They were more nervous than I was. I put them in my pockets.

We got there. Grandmother banged the front door with the iron knocker. The knocking reverberated through the whole house. It was a somewhat unusual-looking house, with many gable-ends and overhanging eaves. It seemed to me to be dripping with sleep.

Grandmother knocked again. We heard no footsteps inside. But the door opened by itself. Someone, perhaps Dino Çiço himself, had lifted the latch with a string from upstairs. Our house also had a cord like that to open the door without going down. We went up the wooden spiral staircase. The scrubbed boards creaked, but the sound was different from the creaking of our own stairs. They spoke a language I didn't know.

When we first went into the living room I didn't see anything, because I was hiding behind Grandmother's skirt. Then I peeked out and saw with one eye some old women dressed in black like Grandmother sitting on the cushions of the wooden ledges that ran around the room. The plane was in the middle. About the size of a person, all white, its wings spread. White. The wings, tail and body were wooden. Screw heads shone on the finely sanded carpentry.

I stared at it for a long time. The voices of the women came from afar, as if through a whistling wind. Then I looked up and saw the pallid man with his red and dreamy eyes turned to the floor.

"Is that him?" I whispered to Grandmother. She nodded.

The old women were chatting in pairs, sipping coffee. Their conversations sometimes got tangled with each other. They kept shaking their heads, expressing their amazement, gesturing in the direction of the plane, then going back to their talk of the war and the bombing. The pallid man did not speak. He never took his eyes off the wooden plane.

"Study hard, little lad, so that one day you'll be as wise as Dino and bring honour to us all," one of the old women said.

I moved farther behind Grandmother. I don't know why, but I felt no joy. It had oozed out of me as if through hundreds of little holes. But that didn't last long. The empty space left in my body by departing joy was suddenly filled with something that flooded in through those same invisible holes. It was sadness. All at once the white plane in the middle of the room seemed to me the frailest, most pitiful thing in the world. How could it dare challenge the huge metal planes that flew overhead every day, those terrifying grey planes loaded with bombs and shaking with deafening noise? It would take them no more than a second to shatter this little white thing, like wild beasts tearing a lamb to pieces.

The old women went on chatting about all sorts of things. The lady of the house offered them more coffee. The pallid man hadn't moved. I stood there too, still dazed. Very slowly, my sorrow gave way to complete indifference. I started looking at the old women's wrinkles and was soon thoroughly absorbed by this new game. I had never examined old people's wrinkles so carefully. How strange they were. They went on and on along an endless winding path from under the chin, down the neck, back up the nape and all over the face. They looked like the threads of wool that Grandmother spun from her distaff at the beginning of winter. Maybe you could knit socks with them, or even pullovers. I was getting very sleepy.

When we left Dino Çiço's house, the rain had stopped. The wet cobblestones gleamed sardonically. They knew something. Two women leaning on their window-ledges chatted across the street. Farther on, three others were doing the same. They were shouting because their windows were far apart, so I heard the news too: an anti-aircraft battery had arrived.

That Sunday afternoon the bells of the two churches rang longer than usual. There were more people in the streets. Harilla Lluka went from door to door shouting: "It's come, it's come!"

"Will you shut up?" an old woman yelled. "We heard already!"

"Those planes are done for now," Bido Sherifi said at the café, where he was having a drink with Avdo Babaramo, who was talking about gunnery. Half the men in the café were listening in awe.

"Gunnery," sighed Avdo. "You don't have the head for it, Bido. But where can I find anyone smart enough to understand?"

All afternoon people came to their windows or onto balconies hoping to get a look at the anti-aircraft battery. Most people looked towards the citadel, certain that the new cannon would be installed up there, as the old anti-aircraft gun had been. But evening fell and there was no sign of any gun barrels. Some said that the battery had been hidden on the outskirts of the city. People were disappointed. They had expected to see gigantic guns with long barrels set up right in the middle of the city, as befitted weapons on which the city relied for its defence. But all they had, it seemed, was a battery hidden far away behind hills and bushes.

"Now in my day we had real artillery," Avdo Babaramo said, raising his last glass in the café.

After this initial disappointment, however, the very secrecy surrounding the anti-aircraft battery seemed to inspire confidence among some people.

Everyone was eager to see its first battle with the bombers. People anxiously awaited the next day, when the bombing would start.

Monday dawned. But strangely enough, the British didn't come that day.

"The swine must have heard about our battery," Harilla Lluka shouted round town. "Those cowards, they must have heard . . ."

"Stop braying like an ass, you idiot."

". . . the louts."

But on Tuesday they came. The siren, as usual, wailed at the sky. Forgetting their earlier impatience, people now rushed downstairs into our cellar. Harilla Lluka was as pale as a sheet.

We heard the menacing, monotonous drone of the engines. Harilla felt that the planes were looking for him personally because he had insulted them so viciously the day before. The noise came closer. Everyone listened open-mouthed.

"It's started, do you hear?" someone said.

"Quiet!"

"Listen! It's firing!"

"Yes, it's definitely firing."

A continuous rumble came from the distance.

"The battery!"

"Why isn't it louder?"

"It's stopped."

"No, there it goes again."

"Why can't we hear it properly?"

"Who knows? Modern weaponry!"

"When the old anti-aircraft gun fired, the whole earth trembled."

"When was that?"

"In the old days."

"Quiet!"

The rumble of the cannon drowned out the drone of the engines for a moment, but then the roar of the planes came through again, louder, more threatening. They sounded angry. A hush fell over the shelter. The sound of the gun couldn't be made out any more. The planes howled savagely. Their shrieks shot into the ground like huge, pitiless stakes. The earth shook. Once. Twice. Three times. As usual.

"They're leaving."

Our battery, which had in fact never stopped firing, could now be heard again. Then suddenly, in the midst of the sadness caused by the defeat of the battery in its first duel and the thought that nothing had changed, came a wild cry from the street outside:

"It's on fire, it's on fire!"

For the first time people ran out into the street before the all-clear had sounded. The streets, windows and court-yards were crammed with heads bobbing madly up and down to see, see, see.

"Look!"

It was white and in its wake a long and fatal plume spread majestically in the wind. It was falling across the sky, and the plane, with its pilot who would be dead in a few seconds, drifted steadily down and disappeared over the horizon. An explosion ripped the air.

The sinister grey plume still hung over the city. As people shouted, howled and cursed, the north breeze, now gathering strength, twisted the smoke in two or three places and finally broke the plume into little pieces. The fragments billowed over the city for a long time.

The crowds of people filling the streets and squares began to move. A throng raced towards the northern edge of the city, where the plane must have crashed. Those who stayed behind came to their windows or climbed up courtyard walls and onto rooftops to watch the crowd, which had passed Varosh Street and was now streaming into Zalli Street. Moments later, the head of the cortège was lost in the distance. Its tail stretched out endlessly.

It was dinner time, but no one budged from the windows and walls until shouts were heard, "They're coming back, they're coming back!" And so they were. First they were seen at the end of Zalli Street, then they spread out over waste ground, and finally reappeared in Varosh Street. The crowd had become a horde lurching forward drunkenly. Kids ran alongside and up ahead of it bearing the latest news.

"They're bringing it, they're bringing it," they shrieked.

"Bringing what?" idlers inquired.

"The arm. The arm."

"What did you say? Speak up."

"They're bringing the arm."

"What arm?"

"Did you hear? They're bringing something. But what? I didn't understand."

"An arm."

"An arm of the plane? Planes have wings, not arms."

The windows, balconies, walls, chimneys and roofs swarmed with people leaning out to get a better view. You could already hear the hum of the advancing crowd. It was getting closer. The din blanketed everything.

At last the horde arrived. It was a truly unbelievable sight. Aqif Kashahu, drenched in sweat, with his eyes bulging and hair over his eyes, was in the lead. He held aloft a cold, wax-like, off-white object.

In the streets there was pandemonium.

"It's a man's arm!"

"The pilot's arm."

"The arm of an Englishman. The arm was all that was left."

"The hand that dropped the bombs."

"The swine."

"The poor Englishman."

"How horrible! Close your eyes!"

Aqif Kashahu kept waving the severed arm for all to see. The hand stayed open.

"Look, he has a ring."

"Look, he has a ring on his finger."

"A ring. You're right. A ring on his finger."

Now and then Aqif Kashahu let out frightful cries. People around him tried to take the arm away from him, but he wouldn't let go for anything in the world.

His wife, watching from a window, began wailing and tearing at her hair.

"Aqif, please, I beg you, throw it away, drop it, it's the devil's claw, drop it!"

Someone fainted.

"Take the children away!" someone shouted.

"God save us!"

"The poor Englishman."

The crowd was moving away towards the centre of the city. The pilot's severed arm, the arm that had struck the city, swayed ghoulishly over people's heads.

FRAGMENT OF A CHRONICLE

ive office. Property. The endless Angoni vs Karllashi case, suspended because of the bombing, resumed yesterday. The first aircraft was shot down over our city. The English pilot's arm was recovered. Never had the city seen such a macabre sight. The crowd held the severed arm aloft. They had seized the ungraspable, the incarnation of evil, the very hand of the cruel fate that had pounded us mercilessly for days. Detailed reports in the next issue. Linguistic column. The gentlemen destroying our language have gone too far in their audacity this time, replacing the beautiful Albanian words for various devices with foreign terms, such as "submarine" and "aircraft." Shameful. Those killed in the latest bombing include: L. Tashi, L. Kadare,

VIII

The siren didn't go off. The guns of the battery didn't fire as usual, nor did the old anti-aircraft unit. But the rumbling of engines thundered so loud that it seemed the sky would collapse. People ran for the shelters and waited to find out what was happening. The noise of the planes got louder and louder.

"What's going on?"

"Why aren't they dropping their bombs?"

It went on for some time. Who knows how long we would have stayed down there if we hadn't heard that almost joyful voice at the top of the stairs.

"Come out, come out and look."

We went out. We could hardly believe our eyes. The sky teemed with planes. They looped over the city like storks, then, one after another, peeled away and came in to land at the airfield.

Taking the stairs four at a time, I ran up the two flights to get a better look. I put the lens over one eye and sat by the window. The view was magnificent. The field below was filling with planes. Their gleaming white wings flashed as they slowly lined up in rows. I had never seen anything so captivating in my life. More beautiful than a dream.

I spent the whole morning watching everything that was happening at the aerodrome: the planes landing, the way they formed up, the patterns they made on the field.

That afternoon Ilir came over.

"Isn't it terrific?" he said. "Now we have our own planes."

"It'll be great!" I said.

"We're *formidable* now, we really are. We'll bomb other cities just like they've been bombing us."

"They'd better watch out!"

"We're *formidable* now," Ilir said again. He had learned the word two days before and liked it a lot.

"You bet!"

"And you said we'd be better off with no sky at all," said Ilir. "Now do you see what we would have lost?"

"You're right."

We chatted for a long time about the aerodrome and the planes. But our enthusiasm was somewhat dampened by other people's sullenness. To our surprise, most people not only failed to rejoice at the arrival of all the planes, but actually seemed irritated by it. Some of them got even angrier about Italy and the Italians.

The nights were black. After dinner, we would all sit by the windows in the main room staring into the darkness. Sometimes the searchlight from the bank of the Zalli groped towards the city through the shadows, extending its beam like a snail putting out its horns. Then we would crouch down below the windowsills and wait silently for the light to reach and then move beyond the front of our house. But most nights were pitch black and we could see nothing, not even one another.

On other nights, army convoys passed along the north-south road, apparently headed for the front. My father would count the pairs of lights, and I would drift off to sleep as I listened to his tally: 122, 123, 124 . . .

For the past few days, I had been in a mood because they wouldn't let us play in the street on account of the threat of bombs. Every morning I would sit at the big windows and carefully observe everything happening on the rooftops. But of course not much ever goes on there. The flocks of crows in the sky only made the tedium of the view worse. The variations in the colour of smoke from the chimneys was just about the only thing worth watching, especially on windy days. A real chimney fire was an almost impossible dream in that season, when people were just starting to use their fireplaces again, and few chimneys had built up enough soot to catch fire properly.

During the day there was very little traffic on the road along the river. Yet the roadway attracted me. I created the missing traffic myself, since if there's one thing a road needs, it's coming and going.

I had heard that the First Crusade had passed this way a thousand years before. Old Xivo Gavo, they said, had related this in his chronicle. The crusaders had marched down the road in an endless stream, brandishing their arms and crosses and ceaselessly asking, "Where is the Holy Sepulchre?" They had pressed on south in search of that tomb without stopping in the city, fading away in the same direction the military convoys were now taking.

A very long time later a lone traveller passed along that same road. He was an Englishman, like the pilot whose severed arm had been placed in the city museum a week before. He composed verses and walked with a limp. He had left his country to wander forever without respite. Hobbling along, he ate up roads and highways. He turned to look at our city as he passed, but didn't stop. He went off in the same direction as the crusaders. They say he was seeking not Christ's tomb but his own.

I peopled the road with crusaders and the lone lame traveller, and enlivened it with a lot of events. I had the crusaders turn back and had them cross swords, sent them a messenger announcing that the Holy Sepulchre had been found, and saw them dash off like one man to go and re-open the tomb. The moment they disappeared, the lone lame man came by. He hobbled on, ever on, and never stopped.

I had spent hours tormenting the road, the crusaders and the crippled Englishman.

But now that was all over. Now I had the airfield, alive and bustling, reaching into the sky and bearing death. I loved it from the very beginning, and felt ashamed that I had ever been sorry the cows were gone.

Dawn. And there it was, shining like nothing else in the world. It looked as if a thousand Kako Pinos had polished to a sheen. It breathed heavily, like a hundred lions, and the sound of its panting rose to the sky. A patch of fog hung over it as if it were paralysed.

"Italy is showing its claws," my younger aunt was telling my father. She glanced at the field with a serious look in her beautiful eyes.

I could not understand how people could not like something as beautiful as the aerodrome. But I had lately become convinced that in general people were pretty boring. They liked to moan for hours on end about how hard it was to make ends meet, about the money they owed, the price of food, and other similar worries, but the minute some more brilliant or attractive subject came up, they were struck deaf.

I left to avoid hearing any more abuse of the aerodrome. I was bewitched. By now I knew everything that went on there. I could tell the difference between the heavy bombers and the light, and between the bombers and the fighters. Every morning I counted the planes, and watched the take-offs, flights and landings. I soon figured out that the bombers never went up by themselves, but were always escorted by fighters. I had given names to some planes that stood out from the rest, and I had some favourites. Whenever I saw some bomber take off with its fighter escort and disappear into the depths of the valley to the south, where they said the war was going on, I kept careful track and waited for it to come back. I worried when one of my favourites was late, and was filled with joy when I heard the humming of engines in the valley announcing its return. Some never came back. I would be sorry for a while, but eventually forgot about it.

So it was that the days went by. I was absorbed by the aerodrome and I thought of nothing else.

One morning I was struck by something unusual the moment I had taken my seat by the window. There on the field, sitting among the planes I knew so well, was a new arrival. I had never seen one so large. The visitor, which had apparently come in during the night, stood there majestically, its light grey wings outstretched. I fell under its spell at once. I forgot all about its colleagues, which looked dwarfed beside it, and welcomed it warmly. Earth and sky together could not have sent me a more beautiful gift than this gigantic plane. It became my best friend. It was my very own flying and roaring machine that put death at my command.

I thought about it all the time. I felt proud to see it take off with a rumble that shook the world and that it alone could make, and to watch it turn slowly south. I never worried so much when any other plane was late coming back in. It always seemed to me that it stayed too long down there in the south. I thought I could hear it breathe heavily on its return. It seemed exhausted. At times like that I would wish it would never fly south again where they were fighting. The others are younger, let them go, I thought. The big one needed some rest.

But it couldn't rest. Heavy and majestic, it took off almost every day and headed for the front. I was sorry not to be down south too, so I could see its huge wings above me.

"Those accursed planes are off again," Grand-mother said one day, standing at the window and pointing at three of them, my great friend among them.

"What have you got against them?" I asked.

"They bring fire and blood wherever they go."

"But the ones here never bomb us."

"They bomb other cities. It's the same thing."

"Which ones?" I asked. "Where?"

"Far away, beyond the clouds," said Grandmother.

I looked in the direction Grandmother had pointed to and said nothing. There beyond the clouds, I thought, far off, there are other cities where they're fighting. What were they like, those other cities? And what was the war like there?

A north wind blew. The big window panes rattled. The sky was overcast. A low and even hum rose up from the aerodrome. Zzz! It filled the valley, coming in waves, never stopping. Zzz-sss. The sound spread and spread. Suzana! What was the secret of your lightness? Butterfly, stork-butterfly. You don't know anything about the aerodrome. At your place now it's like a desert. Blow wind, blow, on and on. Plane-stork-butterfly. Where are you flying off to? Planes hover in the sky . . .

I was awakened by Grandmother's hand on my shoulder.

"You'll catch cold," she said.

I had fallen asleep with my head on the windowsill.

"They've addled your mind," said Grandmother.

It was true. I was bewitched. And cold too.

"The cursed things are off again."

I didn't answer back. I knew she hated them, but that afflicted me now only in respect of the big plane. Maybe Grandmother was right about the others. Who could tell what the planes were doing way down there beyond the clouds, hidden from view? We too stole corn when we went to the fields outside the city, and got up to all kinds of mischief we would never have dared to do in town.

But there was one thing I just couldn't work out — why the opening of the aerodrome had done nothing to stop the bombing. On the contrary, it got worse. When the English planes came, the small fighters took off right away, but the big plane sat on its belly on the field. Why didn't it take off? The idea would torment me. I did all I could to think of excuses, refusing to believe that it could be afraid. No, this plane could never feel fear. During the bombings, as we burrowed in the cellar and it stood out in the middle of the open field, I dreamed for it to take off, just once. The English bombers would turn tail then!

But the big plane was never in the air when the English came; it never took off then. It seemed it would never fly over our city. It knew only one direction, south, where they said the war was raging.

One day I was over at Ilir's. We were playing with the globe, turning it this way and that, when Javer and Isa came in. They were furious, railing at everything, cursing the Italians and the aerodrome and denouncing Mussolini, who was supposed to be coming to visit the city soon. There was nothing unusual about that. Everyone cursed the Italians. We had long known that they were evil, despite their beautiful clothes, their plumes and their shiny buttons. But we didn't know what to think of their planes yet.

"But what are their planes like?" I asked.

"Bastards, just like they are," said Javer.

"You don't understand such things," said Isa. "You're still too young. You'd do better not to ask."

They exchanged a few words in a foreign language, the way they always did when they didn't want us to understand them.

Javer looked at me for a minute, half smiling.

"Your grandmother tells me you really like the aerodrome," he said.

I blushed.

"You like planes, do you?" he asked a moment later.

"Yes, I like them," I said almost spitefully.

"Me too," said Ilir.

They said something else in their unknown language. They didn't seem angry any more. Javer took a deep breath.

"Poor kids," he muttered. "Fallen in love with war, they have. Terrible."

"Sign of the times," Isa said. "This is the age of the plane."

"Did you hear?" asked Ilir. "We're *terrible*."

"*Extraordinarily* terrible," I said. I took the lens out of my pocket and put it over one eye.

"Could you get me a lens like that too?" asked Ilir.

Javer's words stuck in my mind all afternoon. Although when Ilir and I were alone again we decided that what they had said about the planes was a "hateful slander," they had nevertheless cast a shadow of doubt over the aerodrome. Only the big plane was free of all suspicion. Even if all the other planes were evil, my plane couldn't be. I still loved it just as much. My heart swelled with pride when I saw it lift off the runway, filling the valley with its impressive din. I especially loved it when it came back exhausted from the south, where there was fighting.

The nights were terribly dark again. We stayed in the main room two flights up, and my father's monotonous voice once again tallied the lights of the military convoy, now going the opposite way, from south to north. I gazed off into the distance as before, but now I knew that down at the foot of the city, somewhere on the night-drowned field, the big plane was sleeping, its wings outstretched. I tried to figure out the approximate direction of the aerodrome, but it was so dark that I was disoriented. You couldn't see anything at all.

The convoys kept rolling north. The booming of artillery

seemed to come closer every night. The streets and windows were bursting with news.

One morning, we saw long columns of Italian soldiers retreating along the road. They trudged slowly northward, in a direction neither the crusaders nor the lame wanderer had ever taken. Their weapons were slung on their shoulders, and they carried packs on their backs. Here and there among the soldiers were long mule trains loaded with supplies and ammunition.

North . . . Everything was now heading north. It was as if the world had changed direction. (Whenever I turned the globe in one direction, Isa, just to annoy me, would spin it the opposite way. What was happening now was more or less the same.) The defeated Italians were retreating. We expected the Greeks to follow on their tail.

I pressed my nose on the windowpane and concentrated hard on watching the columns move along the road. The little raindrops that the wind now and then battered on the windowpane made it all seem even sadder. The retreat went on all morning. At noon the columns of troops were still marching by. In the afternoon, when the last of them had disappeared beyond the Zalli and the road lay deserted (it was the time when the lame traveller was set to reappear), the air was suddenly filled with the dull growl of engines. I gave a start, as if shaken from a dream. Why? What was going on? In an instant I was no longer sleepy. Something unbearable was happening: they were all taking off! Two at a time, or three by three, the bombers were leaving the airfield with a fighter escort and flying away in that detestable direction, north. Scarcely had one group of three lifted off when another came rumbling down the runway. One after another the clouds swallowed them up. The aerodrome was emptying out. Then I heard the massive noise of the big plane, and my heartbeat slowed. It was all over. For good. It raised itself heavily, turned its beak north and flew off on outstretched wings. Gone forever. From the far horizon bedecked with a thick mist which soon swallowed up the great plane came the last sound of the throaty breathing I knew so well, but it had already grown distant and alien. Suddenly the world sank back into silence.

When I looked beyond the river, I saw that nothing was left. There was just an ordinary field in the autumn rain. The aerodrome had disappeared. My dream had ended.

"What's wrong, my boy?" Grandmother asked when she found me with my head lying like a wrecked ship on the windowsill.

I didn't answer.

Papa and Mamma also came in from the other room and asked me the same question. I wanted to tell them, but my mouth, lips and throat refused to obey. Instead of words, only a hoarse, inhuman sob came out. My parents frowned with fear.

"You're crying for that . . . for that accursed thing whose name I can't even bring myself to say," Grandmother said, pointing towards the field, now splattered with puddles like so many wounds.

"You're snivelling because of the aerodrome?" my father asked angrily. I nodded. He scowled.

"Poor little fool," my mother said. "And I thought you were sick."

They sat in the main room for a long while, torturing

me with their silence. In vain I tried to stifle my sobs. My father's face was glum. Mamma looked lost. Only Grandmother moved back and forth behind me, constantly muttering.

"Lord, what times have come upon us. Kids crying because of those flying things. Evil omens, evil omens."

What was that longing that filled the rain-drenched days? The abandoned field lay below, riddled with small puddles. Sometimes I thought I could hear the sound of it. I would run to the window, to find nothing on the horizon but useless clouds.

Maybe they had shot it down and now it languished on a hillside with its broken wings folded underneath. Once I had seen the remains of a long-limbed bird in a field. Its delicate bones had been washed clean by the rain. Part of it was spattered with mud.

Where could it be?

Over the field, once bound to the sky, a few wisps of fog now drifted.

One day they brought the cows back, and they moved slowly with their silent brown spots, seeking the last bits of grass along the edges of the concrete runway. For the first time I hated them.

The city, weary and sullen, had changed hands several times. The Italians and Greeks alternated. Flags and currencies were changed, amid general indifference. Nothing else.

FRAGMENT OF A CHRONICLE

changing of currencies. The Albanian lek and Italian lira will no longer be accepted. Henceforth the only legal tender will be the Greek drachma. The time limit for the changeover is one week. Yesterday the prison was emptied. The inmates, after thanking the Greek authorities, went their separate ways. I order the cessation of the blackout, effective today. I declare a state of siege, and a curfew from 1800 to 0600 hours. Commander of the city garrison: Katantzakis. Births. Marriages. Deaths. D. Kasoruho and I. Grapshi are happy to

FRAGMENT OF A CHRONICLE

der: restoration of the blackout for the entire city and cancellation of the state of siege. I order the re-opening of the prison. All former inmates are hereby called upon to return to serve out their sentences. Commander of the city garrison: Bruno Arcivocale. Currency must be converted quickly. The Greek drachma is no longer acceptable. The Albanian lek and the Italian lira shall be the sole legal tender. List of those killed in yesterday's bombing: B. Dobi, L. Maksuti, S.

IX

The last Italians left during the first week of November, four days after the evacuation of the aerodrome. For forty hours there was no government in the city. The Greeks arrived at two in the morning. They stayed for about seventy hours, and hardly anyone even saw them. All shutters stayed closed. No one went out in the street. The Greeks themselves seemed to move only at night. At ten in the morning on Thursday the Italians came back, marching in under freezing rain. They stayed only thirty hours. Six hours later the Greeks were back. The same thing happened all over again in the second week of November. The Italians came back. This time they stayed about sixty hours. The Greeks rushed back in as soon as the Italians had gone. They spent all day Friday and Friday night in the city, but when dawn broke on Saturday, the city awoke to find itself completely deserted. Everyone had gone. Who knows why the Italians didn't come back? Or the Greeks? Saturday and Sunday went by. On Monday morning footsteps echoed in the street where none had been heard for several days. On either side of the street women opened their shutters gingerly and looked out. It was Llukan the Jailbird, with his old brown blanket slung over his right shoulder. In his kerchief he was carrying bread and cheese, and was apparently on his way home.

"Llukan!" Bido Sherifi's wife called from a window.

"I was up there," said Llukan, pointing to the prison. "I went there to report, but guess what? The prison is closed."

There was almost a touch of sadness in his voice. The frequent changes of rulers had made mincemeat of his sentence, and this put him out of sorts.

"No more Greeks or Italians, you mean?"

"Greeks, Italians, it makes no difference to me," Llukan answered in exasperation. "All I know is the prison isn't working. The doors are wide open. Not a soul around. It's enough to break your heart."

Someone asked him another question, but he didn't answer and just went on cursing.

"Lousy times, lousy country! Can't even keep a lousy prison running. Am I supposed to waste time every day, climbing up to the citadel and coming back down for nothing? Days go by and I can't serve my damn sentence. All my plans are screwed up. Son of a bitch good for nothing Italy! Damn, when I think about what a friend told me about Scandinavian prisons! Now that's what you call prisons. You go in and out on schedule, by the book. Fixed sentences and good records. The gates don't swing open and shut all the time like the doors of a whorehouse."

One by one, the women closed their shutters as Llukan got more and more obscene. Only Aqif Kashahu's mother, who was deaf, stayed at her window and answered what she thought she was hearing.

"How true, dear fellow, how true. You've every right to be angry, my boy. Never had a lucky day in your life, poor thing, rotting in prison all the time. Governments come and go, and you're always inside."

Llukan the Jailbird walked on and the street was empty again. Nazo's big cat leaped across the cobblestones. Kako Pino's new cat, which had climbed up on the porch, sat and watched him. Around noon a stray dog passed by. All afternoon there was not a soul to be seen, apart from a solitary chicken.

The next morning, as Llukan the Jailbird came swearing down from the prison again with his blanket over his shoulder and kerchief-wrapped bread in hand, everyone finally got the idea that a period of no government had begun.

The first doors were opened just a slit. Little by little, the street came back to life. Some people ventured into the city centre. The Addis Ababa Café re-opened. The wind scattered newspaper shreds in the square. Empty tins lay here and there. The town hall looked sullen, with all its doors and windows boarded up. People strolled around, eyeing empty crates with Latin or Greek letters painted in black on their boards. The pedestal of the city's only monument had been plastered with notices issued by the Italian and Greek garrison commanders. The posters were all torn. Someone was carefully gathering up random pieces: "XAQIS," "KAT," "Q," "NX." His collar was turned up, and he kept shaking his head, perhaps because he couldn't find all the words. The cold wind blew the shreds from his hands.

These posters, turned to scraps by wind and rain, were all that remained of the turmoil of recent days. The city had been left without a government. In quick succession it had lost the planes, the anti-aircraft guns, the siren, the brothel, the searchlight and the nuns.

Briefly seduced by adventure, and having had a taste of the sky and of international dangers, the city had been stunned by it all and now withdrew into its ancient stones. Wind and rain were now vying to anaesthetise its jagged nerves. It was dazed. Its links to the sky had been permanently severed. The foreign planes that passed overhead no longer recognised it, or pretended not to see it. They flew high, leaving behind only a disdainful rumble.

One morning, after carefully closing the door behind her, Kako Pino went out into the street.

"Where are you off to, Kako Pino?" Bido Sherifi's wife asked from her window.

"To a wedding."

"A wedding? Who's got it into his head to get married in times like these?"

"People marry in all kinds of times," Kako Pino said.

The fact that Kako Pino was on her way to a wedding showed that the city could easily cope without a government. But as in any period of transition, these were uncertain times. The normal rules of life were suspended. The newspapers did not come out. No courts were in session. No more announcements, posters or ordinances appeared on the walls of the town hall. News, whether local or foreign, came only by word of mouth. The chief source was an old, hitherto unknown woman whose name suddenly spread far and wide in those faceless days. Her name was Sose, but most people called her "Old News."

Ex-convicts, suspicious-looking men from the Highlands of Labëri, and other strangers wandered through the town. Everything was fleeting, unstable. The squares, streets and telegraph poles hoarded their secrets. Doors were manifestly mistrustful. The days were cold and without substance. Only the chimney stacks were fully alive.

It was then that Xhexho reappeared. The knock at the door fell on my head like a hammer blow. I wanted to hide, disappear, but it was impossible. Up the stairs she came, wheezing as always. Fear, gossip and news scurried before her like little black cats. There was no stopping them.

"Well, it's Xhexho!" Grandmother said.

"Xhexho!" my mother said.

"How are you, Xhexho?" my father asked. "Where have you been all this time?"

Xhexho didn't answer. As always, it was Grandmother she talked to.

"You see, Selfixhe? You see what God has sent us? I told you, Selfixhe, that black water would spurt from the springs. And sure enough, it did. Black. Have you seen the bomb-craters at Hazmurat? And Meçite? And Upper Palorto? Black water everywhere."

"What is this black water?" I whispered to my mother.

"Bombs make craters in the ground, and they fill up with dirty water," she said.

"But these people never learn," Xhexho went on in her rasping, doom-laden voice. "Did you hear what they did? They stole that Englishman's arm from that mu . . . mu- . . . how do you say it?"

"Museum," my father said.

"Stole it, Selfixhe. No more, no less."

"But who? What for?" my mother asked.

"A good question," Xhexho whined. "Because they're possessed, my girl. Because this is the age of the Evil One. Everything is upside down. Heaven dropped that Englishman's arm down on us. Now you'll see German hair and Chinese beards raining down on us, and then nails of Jews and Arabs' noses . . ."

Xhexho went on and on. I stood aside, listening hard and trying to imagine a snowfall of nails, hair, beards and noses. I would ask Grandmother as soon as Xhexho left.

Maksut came by in the street, carrying a head I thought I recognised under his arm. It had been a long time since I'd seen his pretty wife. I would have to wait for spring to see her sitting out on her doorstep again. By this time they must have had a pyramid of severed heads at their house like the ones piled up by Genghis Khan. What was . . . garita doing now, I wondered. (The way she looked, her face, even her name now came to my mind only in part, like a hunk of bread gnawed by rats.)

Xhexho left. At first Qani Kekezi was suspected of stealing the Englishman's arm, but then suspicion fell on Xivo Gavo the chronicler. Others thought it had been a smuggler from Varosh. The rumour was that he had sold the arm to a monastery on the other side of the mountain.

The city busied itself with petty affairs. That good-for-nothing Lame Kereco Spiri wandered the streets drunk, lamenting the passing of the brothel.

"They closed it, they closed it," he kept saying, almost sobbing. "My warm little hearth, my feathered nest. They closed it on me! Woe is me! Where will I lay my head these winter nights?"

From time to time Llukan the Jailbird joined in the lament.

"My warm little hearth, my feathered nest," Llukan would repeat mechanically.

"Get out of here! Have you no shame?" the old ladies shouted at them. "Get out of here!"

"Oh my lost little nest, where have you gone? O *sole mio*," Lame Kareco Spiri mumbled in bewilderment as he blew kisses to the old ladies.

"Get out of here, good for nothing! May lightning strike you, may the earth swallow you up!"

"*Doubt thou the stars are fire; doubt that the sun doth move . . .*"

"Doubt that the sun doth move?" repeated Llukan.

"Go to hell, both of you."

Things had really ground to a halt. People and things seemed to crawl along. Cattle grazed in the aerodrome field. Dino Çiço had suspended his research. His imagination was running dry.

In this somnolent state, the city sought to re-establish contact with the outside world once more. To do so it used the old anti-aircraft gun in the citadel.

This old gun, kept in the citadel's western tower since the days of the monarchy, could be seen from every corner of the city. Its long barrel, seeming slightly tired, pointed permanently at the sky. It was a familiar object as dear to everyone as its neighbour, the old clock, set into the other tower next to it. But with the passing years people had almost forgotten how to make use of that long tube and the handles, gears and winches built into the emplacement. From the time of its dedication (old men could still remember the ceremony organised by the city government, with patriotic speeches, music, bottles of beer and Lamçe the Gypsy who got thoroughly drunk and leapt from the fortress wall to his death in the street) the anti-aircraft gun had never once been fired.

After the bombing started, once people recovered from the initial shock and took cover in the shelters, the memory of the weapon flashed through the back of their minds. They recalled that the long metal tube, the levers and mechanism called "anti-aircraft gun," were meant for just such occasions. It was a kind of revelation and everyone started asking:

"What about our anti-aircraft gun? Why doesn't it come on?"

"You're right, we do have an anti-aircraft gun. Why don't we ever hear it?"

The initial disillusionment with our anti-aircraft defence was bitter indeed. When people came out of the cellars, they looked towards the western tower, where the silhouette of the weary, unmoved barrel stood out against the sky.

"It's an outrage." The expression, which as far as I knew was usually applied to women, and definitely not to weapons, was first uttered in the Addis Ababa Café, and was soon on everybody's lips.

It was outrageous the old gun hadn't been heard . . . If it had been a miserable little fire-cracker or some handgun of the kind infantrymen get as basic equipment, then it might be excused for being scared and upset at the sight of enemy aviation, but that long-limbed monster of a gun had been designed for just such eventualities and could not be forgiven for having let us down.

What people obviously held against it more than anything else was the length of its barrel. When I studied the gun with the help of Grandmother's opera glasses I sometimes imagined I could read its thoughts. You often say of someone accused of a misdeed that he's retreated into his shell, or that he's shrunk away. But that poor gun could not hide or cringe, and had to stay sticking out in full sight of all.

Apparently some people took pity on it just as I did, and tried to invent excuses for it. It was rumoured that it was all the fault of the former mayor, the one who'd been in office at the time of the gun's inauguration. People said he'd sold a key part of the mechanism — the range finder — and spent the proceeds on a wild orgy with a Macedonian whore in the fleshpots of Skopje. So he'd left the unfortunate weapon to cope with hostile skies without a range finder, which was like robbing it of its eyes.

Outrage steadily infiltrated the city. Meanwhile, other folk, of the kind who were utterly intransigent when the city's honour was at stake (as they had been in the case of Argjir Argjiri) had a change of heart. True, there was something wrong with the gun, they said, but the defect had nothing to do with those stories about thieving and Macedonian whores. It was suffering a routine mechanical malfunction of the sort that could afflict materiel in any army in the world. Anyway, hadn't officers of both opposing forces been to examine it, and taken a sceptical attitude towards its potential perform-ance (not to mention the more offensive remarks they had made)? They can keep their opinions to themselves! others retorted. Don't soldiers always bad-mouth their opponents' equipment to make their own seem superior? Sure, armies have problems, but so do cities. Let others tear themselves to pieces with whatever weapons they want. But the city had to defend itself, by its own means. If all it had to fight with were lances — even if all it had were medieval pikestaffs! — then so be it! Because when all's said and done, this was a matter of honour . . .

By the end of a day, during which the arguments had gone back and forth, the view that the gun should be repaired finally prevailed. A procession consisting of a municipal mechanic, two of the town's best clockmakers, Xivo Gavo the chronicler, the former artillery man Avdo Babaramo, a priest who had been unfrocked barely two weeks before and who claimed to have been a number in a gun crew in the First World War and to have even shot down a Turkish plane, and Qani Kekezi, whose presence had led Dino Çiço to change his mind and stay at home at the last minute, wound its way up to the citadel and its tower.

The whole city waited, holding its breath. Women were asking from the windows:

"Is it fixed?"

"Not yet."

"Lord help us."

Everyone was asking that question, morning, noon and especially towards evening. The defect was apparently serious.

That was when the anti-aircraft battery that later shot down the first English plane arrived. Two days later, the old anti-aircraft gun was fired for the first time. The joy felt by everyone, especially the children, was indescribable. Unlike the salvos of the battery, the boom of the old anti-aircraft gun was lonely and powerful. There was really something regal about it. But that day it didn't manage to hit anything. Nor did it make a hit on any subsequent day.

As we sat in the shelter Ilir would say to me, "It's formidable. Today it will get one for sure." But it never did. Every day we would come up out of the shelter gripped by sadness. We would stand close to the grown-ups to hear what they were saying. And what we heard was disheartening. They had no faith in it. After every bombing they would repeat resentfully:

"It's too old to shoot down today's planes."

Over the preceding weeks, when the city had repeatedly changed hands, our anti-aircraft gun had missed every shot. During the Italian occupation, it had fired at English planes. When the Greeks came, its targets were the Italian planes that bombed us four times in succession. Neither of the retreating armies had touched the gun. The evacuations were quick and chaotic, and it was too much trouble for either army to dismantle the gun at the top of the fortress. Or perhaps, in their disarray, they forgot it or pretended to forget it, confident that when they had retaken the city they would find the veteran weapon just as they had left it.

On one of those days when the city had no government, an unknown plane was spotted in the sky, coming from a direction from which none had ever come before. Perhaps it was the same bewildered pilot who had flown over last week and dropped leaflets in German that began: "Citizens of Hamburg!"

In recent days the appearance of stray aircraft in the skies over our city had become commonplace. They must have wandered off course after some battle, or were pretending to be off course while flying towards the enemy. Turning from their set itinerary at the earliest opportunity, especially when the weather was bad, they would leave their companions and loop idly in the sky until their flying time was up. They acted pretty much the way we did some mornings when, instead of going to school, we played truant until it was time to go home for lunch.

The unknown aircraft flew slowly, looking weary and bored. It must have been coming out of some battle, even though the direction it came from seemed suspect. Later on, trying to figure out why the bemused pilot had suddenly dropped a bomb on us, people guessed that he must have noticed that he had one left (usually these stray pilots dropped their bombs deep in the woods or up in the mountains) and must have said to himself, as he flew over, "Well, why not just drop it on this city whose name I don't even know?" And he dropped it.

But this time the city couldn't stand the blow. During the long days of apathy, the long barrel of the old anti-aircraft gun had let its imagination run wild. Its repressed desire to get mixed up in the affairs of the sky was slumbering within it, ready to awaken. And when unknown planes flew over the city, the temptation to open fire at the intruders was particularly strong.

It was one of those rare days when we had gone out to play. We had gone pretty far, to the foot of the citadel, near the isolated house of Avdo Babaramo, the old gunner. Often, in the shelter or the coffeehouse, old Avdo would tell war stories, and though we had never seen anything but pumpkins and cucumbers in his hands, and certainly never cannon shells, he nevertheless enjoyed the respect of all.

We were playing right in front of Avdo's house when we heard the noise of an engine. Some passers-by stopped and, shading their eyes, searched the sky for the plane.

"There it is!" someone said.

"Looks like an Italian plane."

Uncle Avdo and his wife came to the window. Other passers-by had stopped in the street to look.

The plane flew slowly. The lone, loud hum of its engines came in waves. Silence fell over the onlookers. Then suddenly someone turned towards Avdo Babaramo's window and called, "Uncle Avdo, why don't you take a shot with our anti-aircraft gun for once? Shoot that pig looping about up there."

The crowd murmured. As for us kids, our hearts pounded with excitement.

"Yeah, shoot it down, Uncle Avdo!" two or three voices shouted.

"Why provoke the devil?" Uncle Avdo answered from the window. "Leave him alone."

"Come on, Uncle Avdo!" we all cried, "shoot it down!"

"Shut up, you little devils!" someone said. "Quiet!"

"Why should they be quiet? They're right."

"Shoot it down, Avdo. There's the anti-aircraft gun, sitting right up there. Doing nothing."

"Why look for trouble?" asked Harilla Lluka from the middle of the crowd. "Better leave him alone. We'll only make him angry and he'll bomb us to bits."

"We've had enough of that already, son."

At first Avdo Babaramo's face grew dark, but then he brightened up. A thin blue vein stood out on his forehead. He lit a cigarette.

"Shoot it down, Uncle Avdo!" Ilir shouted, almost sobbing.

Suddenly a black object fell away from the belly of the plane, and a few seconds later we heard an explosion.

Then something so wonderful happened that we would have thought it impossible. The angry crowd started shouting, "Shoot the lousy dog down, Avdo!"

Uncle Avdo had walked out to the gate. His eyes flashed. He swallowed repeatedly. His wife followed in alarm. The plane was flying slowly over the city. Somehow Avdo found himself in the midst of the crowd, which pulled him along the steep road leading up to the citadel.

From every side came the cry: "Shoot! Shoot the pig down!"

The path led directly to the tower where the anti-aircraft gun sat. Uncle Avdo, now at the head of the crowd, entered the citadel gates.

"Hurry, Uncle Avdo! Hurry, before it goes!" we kids were shouting.

They didn't let us into the citadel. We stayed outside, clapping our hands impatiently, for the plane was heading off towards the mountains.

"It's going, it's going!" everyone shouted.

But suddenly the plane turned and started coming close again. It really seemed to be flying at random.

Sudden voices rang out from afar: "His glasses! His glasses!"

"Quick, his glasses!"

"Uncle Avdo's glasses!"

Someone tore down the hill and, a moment later, came charging back up just as fast, carrying Uncle Avdo's antique spectacles.

"He's about to shoot!" someone shouted.

"The plane's coming back!"

"Like a lamb to the slaughter."

"Shoot, Uncle Avdo. Blow him away!"

The antique anti-aircraft gun fired. Its sound was no more powerful than our screams. Our hearts were bursting with joy. Everyone was shouting now, even the old ladies.

It fired again. We had expected the plane to come crashing down after the first shot, but no. It continued to fly slowly over the city. It was as if the pilot had dozed off. He was in no hurry.

At the third shot the plane was right over the main square.

"Now he'll get him!" a raucous voice shouted. "There he is, right under our noses!"

"Shoot the lousy dog down!"

"Get the son of a bitch!"

But the plane wasn't hit. It flew off north. The gunner fired a few more rounds before the plane was completely out of range.

"Uncle Avdo hasn't got the hang of it yet," someone said. "It's not his fault. He's used to the old ones."

"What, the Turkish guns?" asked Ilir.

"Maybe."

We sighed. Our throats were parched.

The anti-aircraft gun fired again, but the plane was too far away now. There was a hateful indifference in its flight path.

"The pig's getting away," someone burst out.

Tears welled up in Ilir's eyes. In mine too. When the final shell was fired and the crowd began to disperse, a little girl started sobbing.

The people who had gone up to the tower were coming down now, with Avdo Babaramo in the lead. He was pale. His hands trembled as he mopped his brow with a handkerchief. His haggard gaze wandered, not focusing on anything. Avdo's old wife made her way through the crowd and came up to him.

"Come, my darling," she called. "Come and lie down. You must be exhausted. This is not for you. Not with your heart trouble. Come on."

He wanted to say something, but he couldn't. His mouth was dry. Only when he had crossed the threshold of his gate did he turn to look back. Setting his jaw in a half-smile, half-grimace, he muttered with great effort:

"It was not to be."

The people left.

"It was not to be," the gunner repeated, passing his gaze over all those present as if seeking their approval before they left him alone with his defeat.

"Don't worry about it, Uncle Avdo," a boy told him. "Some day it will be our turn. And we won't miss."

Uncle Avdo closed his door.

The crowd dispersed.

OLD SOSE'S NEWS
(in lieu of a chronicle)

My joints hurt. We will have a hard winter. War has broken out everywhere, a murderous war all the way to the Celestial Kingdom, where the people are yellow. The English are sending banknotes and gold to all countries. Red-bearded Stalin smokes his pipe and ponders, ponders. "You know a lot, Englishman," he says, "but I know just as much as you." "Oh, my dear Hançe," said Majnur, the lady of Kavo, to poor old Hançe the day before yesterday, "when will this war with the Greeks be over? I'm dying for a Lake Ioanina eel." "Enough, wretch," snapped Hançe, "my children are starving and you talk of Ioanina eels." They quarrelled and cursed each other: you ragamuffin, you Italian lackey, you this, you that. As soon as the town hall re-opens, Avdo Babaramo will be fined for firing the gun without authorisation. They say the war with the Greeks will be over before the first mountain snowfall. The Kailis' daughter-in-law is pregnant again. Both of the Puses' daughters-in-law are in their ninth month, as if they had worked it out together. Granny Hava is bed-ridden. "I won't live to see winter," she says. Poor old Lady Qazim finally died too. May the earth be kind to her.

X

It rained all the next day. The city lay stunned after the previous day's defeat, its roofs and eaves drenched. Sadness trickled down the slates. Unyieldingly grey, it slid down the steep roofs, steadily renewed by the fresh sadness that poured from sorrowful reservoirs in the sky.

The next morning the city awoke to find itself occupied again. The Greeks were back. This time their mules, cannon and supplies were everywhere. On the metal pole atop the prison tower, where the Italian tricolour had flown, the Greek flag now waved. At first it was hard to make it out. The wind never stopped blowing, but it never blew in just one direction so that the banner could unfurl and be seen properly. Towards noon, when the wind shifted and the rain started again, the outlines of the large white cross could at last be seen on the weary silk.

"Did I have to live so long just to see Greek jackboots?" Grandmother lamented. "Why didn't I die last winter?"

We were in the main room. I had never seen such despair in her eyes, in all her features. I couldn't think of anything to say to her. I took the round lens from my pocket and put it over one eye. The distant cross over the prison tower fluttered as if it were angry. Then it displayed itself in full, quite brazenly. It was just a pattern on a piece of silk. I wondered how two crossed lines on a piece of fabric could arouse such grief. A piece of material waving in the breeze had plunged an entire city into consternation. It was strange.

That evening people spoke of nothing but the Greeks. Terrible predictions were made. Many years ago, before the monarchy and even before the republic, the Greeks had occupied the city for a few weeks. Many people had been killed. Then as now, that same flag with the white cross had flown from the prison tower. And since the flag with the cross was back, all the rest would follow.

Xivo Gavo's little window stayed lit far into the night. The old chronicler's neighbours all thought he was describing the return of the Greeks. It later turned out that he had devoted only a single sentence of his chronicle to the event: "On 18 Nov. the G. entered the city." No one could account for this laconic mention of such a calamity, and still less for his use of a single letter to represent the multitude of Greeks.

The next morning the cross was still there, dominating the city. The symbol of evil had been raised. Everyone expected the worst.

The Greeks began to walk around the streets in their khaki uniforms. Ordinances signed "Katantzakis" were again posted in the square. The coffee houses were packed with Greek sounds. They were thin and sharp, full of s's and th's that cut like razors. All the soldiers carried knives. Treachery hovered in the air. Impending slaughter. The city would have to be sluiced with a rubber hose. But it was raining. Maybe they wouldn't need the hose.

There was no massacre on the first day. Nor on the second. They had put a big sign in the town square saying *Vorio Epire*, "Northern Epirus." Commandant Katantzakis lunched and dined with some of the rich Christian families.

A Greek sergeant fired several shots, but no one was hit. He did, however, get the city's only statue in the thigh. It was a big bronze statue in the town square, erected back in the days of the monarchy. The city had never had statues before that. The only representations of the human form were the scarecrows in the fields on the other side of the river. When plans to put up a statue were announced, many fanatical citizens who had hailed the anti-aircraft gun had been somewhat sceptical. A metal man? Was such a novelty really necessary? Might it not cause trouble? At night, when everyone was sleeping as God had ordained, the statue would be out there standing erect. Day and night, summer and winter, it would stand. People laughed and cried, shouted and died. But not the statue. It would just stand there and not utter a sound. And everyone knew how suspicious silence was.

The sculptor who came from Tirana to inspect the proposed site of the pedestal barely escaped blows. A bitter polemic raged in the city newspaper. At last the majority of the population resigned itself to having the statue. It arrived in a huge lorry with a tarpaulin over the back. It was winter. They set it up at night in the main square. To avoid trouble there was no unveiling ceremony. People stood and stared in wonder at the bronze warrior with his hand on his pistol, who gazed severely down into the square as if asking, "Why didn't you want me?"

One night someone threw a blanket over the bronze

man's shoulders. From then on, the city's heart went out to its statue.

Anyway, this was the statue the Greek sergeant shot. People rushed to the square to see the bullet hole. Some of them went starry-eyed and imagined that they themselves had to limp. Others actually were limping, as if they had been hit in the thigh. The square was in turmoil. Suddenly Katantzakis, escorted by several guards, appeared at the edge of the square, walked across it diagonally, and went into the town hall, where the Greek command was headquartered.

An hour later, in the spot reserved for proclamations, a sign was posted, in Greek and Albanian and signed by Katantzakis, ordering the arrest of the sergeant who had shot the statue.

That afternoon Xhexho came over.

"Oh my poor dears, do you know what we're in for now?" she cried the moment she came through the door. "They say Vasiliqia has come back."

"Vasiliqia?" exclaimed Grandmother, going pale.

"Vasiliqia?" my mother repeated in horror.

My father, hearing their voices, came in from the other room.

"What's this, Xhexho? Vasiliqia's back?"

There was a pause during which all you could hear was Xhexho's wheezy breathing.

"If only I had died last winter," lamented Grandmother. "Under the earth I would be spared such things."

"I should have been so lucky," Xhexho agreed.

"I thought nothing in this life could surprise me any more," Grandmother said, "but Vasiliqia coming back?

Anything but that." There was a terrifying resignation in her voice.

Papa cracked his long sinewy fingers.

"They say she's worse than ever now," Xhexho went on. "It will be a catastrophe."

"Woe betide us," my mother wailed.

"Where is she?" my father asked. "When will we see her?"

"She's locked up in Pasha Kauri's house. They're just waiting for the right day to bring her out."

There was a knock at the door. It was Bido Sherifi's wife, along with Kako Pino, Nazo's daughter-in-law (more beautiful than ever amidst these horror-struck faces), and Mane Voco's wife, holding Ilir by the hand.

"Vasiliqia?"

"Is it true? She's back?"

"How dreadful!"

All the old women had facial tics. Their wrinkles leapt about so furiously it seemed they would come loose and fall off. I had the feeling I was already entangled in those wrinkles.

"So it is, Selfixhe," said Xhexho, folding her arms on her chest.

"You've brought us tidings of death, Xhexho."

"The end of the world."

I had already heard about Vasiliqia. The name of this woman, who had terrorised our city some twenty years before, was linked in my mind with words like "cholera," "plague" and "calamity," and like them, cropped up in most of the curses people levelled at one another. For long years the name Vasiliqia had hung over their heads like an ever-present threat. Now it had stepped forward out of the universe of words and was plummeting down upon us, assuming the body, eyes, hair and mouth of a woman dressed in black.

More than twenty years ago this woman had arrived in our city with the Greek occupation forces. She would wander the streets in the company of a patrol of Greek gendarmes, weapons at the ready. "That man there has the evil eye," she would say to them, "seize him." And the gendarmes would grab him. "That boy over there looks suspicious. He's no Christian. Grab him, cut him to pieces and throw him in the river."

She moved through the streets, went into coffee houses, sat staring at people in the main square. The Greeks called her the holy maid. The streets and coffee houses emptied out. She was shot at twice, but was not hit. More than a hundred men and boys were executed on her orders. Then one fine day she walked off with a column of soldiers, heading south, back where she came from.

The city had never forgotten her. Once she had left the real world her name, "Vasiliqia," had entered the abstract realm of words. "May the eye of Vasiliqia cut you down," old women would curse. Vasiliqia became more and more remote, as distant as the plague (for plague, too, had once been very near), perhaps even as remote as death. Embittered by her long absence, all of a sudden she had now come back.

Evening fell. Pasha Kauri's windows were draped with blankets. Why hadn't they brought her out? What were they waiting for?

The city kept vigil with Vasiliqia on its mind.

The next day, around mid-morning, Xhexho came over again.

"The streets are deserted," she reported. "Gjergj Pula was

the only one I saw, going up to the market. Did you hear that he's changed his name again?"

"To what?" asked Grandmother.

"Yiorgos Poulos."

"The scoundrel!"

Gjergj Pula lived in a neighbourhood near ours. The first time the Italians came he had changed his name to Giorgio Pulo.

There was a knock at the door. Bido Sherifi's wife came in, followed by Nazo's daughter-in-law.

"We saw Xhexho coming in. Is there any news?"

"Better to be dead and buried than to hear the news there is," said Xhexho. "Have you heard what they're saying about Bufe Hasani?"

Grandmother nodded in my direction. I pretended not to be listening. Whenever Bufe Hasani's name came up, Grandmother was careful not to let me hear.

"He has taken up . . . with a Greek soldier."

"What a disgrace!"

"His wife is beside herself. 'I thought it was all over when the Italians left,' she wept, 'when that damned Pepe took off, stinking of hair-cream from twenty paces. But now that filthy husband of mine has got his hooks into one of those *spiropoules*. A Greek, sisters, a Greek!'"

Nazo's daughter-in-law's almond eyes sharpened. Bido Sherifi's wife pinched her cheeks, leaving traces of flour.

"That Bufe Hasani has his mind made up, and he has the cheek to say so. He says he's going to pick a lover from every occupying army. A German if the Germans come, a Japanese if the Japanese come."

"What about Vasiliqia?"

Xhexho snorted.

"They're keeping her locked up. Who knows what they're waiting for."

In the afternoon Ilir came over.

"Isa and Javer have got revolvers," he told me. "I saw them with my own eyes."

"Revolvers?"

"Yeah. But don't tell anyone."

"What are they going to do with them?"

"They're going to kill people. I was looking through the keyhole and heard them arguing about who they were going to kill first. They're making a list. They're still there in Isa's room, arguing."

"Who are they going to bump off?"

"Vasiliqia first, if she comes out. Javer wanted to put Gjergj Pula second, but Isa was against it."

"That's odd."

"Let's go listen through the keyhole."

"OK."

"Where are you going?" my mother asked. "Don't go too far. You never know, Vasiliqia might come out!"

Isa and Javer had left the door ajar. We went in. They had stopped arguing. Javer was even humming a tune. Apparently they had reached agreement. Isa's glasses looked bigger than usual. The lenses gleamed. They turned to look at us. They had the death list on them. You could tell from the way they looked.

"Can we go out and play," Ilir asked, "or will Vasiliqia come out?"

Isa stared at us, not moving. Javer frowned.

"I don't think they're letting her out," he said. "Her time has passed."

There was a long silence. From the window you could see the road and part of the airfield beyond. The cows were still grazing on it. A vague memory of the big plane came back to me in flashes, as it had already several times. Far above the boring talk of Vasiliqia and the shameful behaviour of Bufe Hasani, its gleaming metal sparkled, so distant that it strained my eyes. That's a point: where was it now? The image of the dead bird with its wings folded under it now mingled in my mind with Suzana's frail, almost transparent limbs, and the three of them together — plane, bird and Suzana — mixing a young girl's flesh, alloy and feathers, swapping life and death, had forged a single and *extraordinary* being.

"Her time has passed," Javer repeated. "You can walk the streets without fear."

We left. The streets were not as empty as Xhexho had said. Çeço Kaili and Aqif Kashahu were tramping over the cobblestones. Çeço Kaili's red hair looked like a flame fanned by the wind. They were often together these days. Perhaps grief at their daughters' disgrace had united them. One day Ilir had heard some women say that for a father, having a daughter who had been kissed by a boy was practically the same thing as having a daughter with a beard.

Both men looked glum. Lady Majnur had come to her window with a twig of marjoram in her hand. The houses of the other ladies which stood beside hers had their windows tightly shut. The Karllashi house, with its massive iron door (the hand-shaped iron knocker reminded me of the English pilot's severed arm), was silent.

"Should we go to the square and see the hole in the statue?" asked Ilir.

"OK."

"Look, Greeks!"

Soldiers were standing around in front of the boards where cinema posters were usually put up. They all had very dark complexions.

"Do the Greeks belong to the gypsies?" Ilir whispered.

"I don't know. I don't think so. None of them has a violin or clarinet."

"Look, that's where Vasiliqia's locked up," Ilir said, pointing at Pasha Kauri's brown-painted house, where some gendarmes were standing guard.

"Don't point," I warned.

"Don't worry," Ilir said. "Her time has passed."

The Addis Ababa Café was closed. The barbershops too. A few more steps and we would cross the square. From afar we could see that the posters at the base of the statue had been torn by the wind. Sss-zzz. I stopped.

"Listen," I said.

Ilir froze, open-mouthed.

A muffled rumble came from the distance. Someone on the square looked up at the sky. A Greek soldier shaded his eyes with his hand.

"Planes," Ilir said.

We were in the middle of the square. The rumble grew louder. Suddenly the square seemed to have become much larger. The Greek soldier shouted out loud, then bolted. The sky trembled so much that I thought it would crumble.

Yes, it was him! His noise. His roar.

"Quick!" screamed Ilir, pulling at my sleeve. "Hurry!"

But I was frozen stiff.

"The big plane," I mumbled in a daze.

"Down!" someone yelled sternly.

The howl was deafening now. It engulfed the sky and smothered the blast of the old anti-aircraft gun, whose shells disappeared into the void.

"Get dow-w-w-n!"

A fragment of a shout reached me from afar, and suddenly I saw, directly overhead, three bombers that had surged up from behind the roofs at dizzying speed. He was one of them. Yes, I would know him anywhere. He was huge, he had his great grey wings all stretched out, he was cruel and blinded by war, and he dropped his bombs: one, two, three . . . Heaven and earth crashed against each other. A blind force hurled me to the ground. Why was he doing it? What for? My ears ached. Enough! I couldn't see anything. No ears, no eyes. I must be dead.

When everything was still again I heard a hoarse sob. It was me, crying . . . I got up. Miraculously, the square was still flat, though just a few moments before it had seemed hopelessly upside down, forever twisted. Ilir was lying face down a few steps away. I went to him, grabbed him by the shoulders, and shook him. He'd grazed the skin on his forehead and hands. I was bleeding, too. Wordless, crying our hearts out, we set out quickly but sadly for home. On Market

Street we ran into Isa and Javer who were running towards us, very pale. When they saw us, they gave a shout and grabbed us in their arms, then ran home with us at the same frenzied pace.

The Italians came back to the city. In the morning the road was filled with mules, guns and endless columns of soldiers. The Greek flag with its white cross was taken down from the prison tower, giving way to the Italian tricolour with its fascist insignia.

It was soon obvious that this was not just another passing occupation. The siren, the searchlight, the anti-aircraft battery, the nuns and the prostitutes all followed the soldiers in. Only the aerodrome stayed empty. Instead of military aircraft just one strange orange plane came to land there. It was ugly, with a flat nose and short wings, and people called it "Bulldog." It looked like an orphan all alone there on the tarmac.

XI

Greece had been defeated. It was snowing. The windowpanes were covered with frost. I stared blankly at the swarms of refugees on the road below. In tatters. Snowflakes and rags. The world seemed filled with them. Somewhere down there lay Greece all in shreds, and in the winter wind its ghostly remnants flitted this way and that like clumps of goose-down or scraps of cloth.

The refugees trudged up the city streets in endless streams. They were all famished and frozen stiff — soldiers and civilians, women carrying babies in wicker baskets, old men, officers without their pips — all pounded on doors in distress, begging for bread.

"*Psomi! Psomi!*"

The haughty city looked down its nose and gazed at the defeated. Its gates were high, its windows out of reach. Pleading voices rose up from below as from the brink of death.

"*Psomi! Psomi!*"

So that's what the rout of a nation looked like. From conversations overheard in the shelter I had gathered that of the countries we knew from our postage stamps only France and Poland had so far suffered defeat. They too must have filled the world with tatters and the word *psomi*. (Ilir told me it was impossible that the French and Poles also called bread *psomi*, but I insisted that all defeated countries called it that.)

Snow covered everything. It was cold. The chimneys smoked steadily. Beneath the heavy roofs, life, disrupted by recent events, settled down again. The Angoni vs Karllashi trial resumed. Llukan the Jailbird, with his blanket over his shoulder and his bread wrapped in a kerchief, crossed the neighbourhood on his way to the prison, greeting passers-by right and left. Lame Kareco Spiri also seemed at ease again. Kako Pino was summoned to a wedding in Dunavat; Nazo's cat disappeared.

Life seemed to be back to normal. The nuns looked even blacker against the snow. The searchlight beamed with new lustre. Only the aerodrome remained deserted. It was utterly empty now. Not even cows. Just snow. I was getting ready to turn the crusaders loose (who would mix with the refugees), and the lame man too. But that very day, just when life seemed to be settling back into its old routine, the bombing started again.

The cellar, which had been abandoned for a while, was now full again. It was warm there in winter.

"Here we are again, flocking like chicks around a hen," said the women, greeting one another as they energetically, almost joyfully, unrolled their blankets and mattresses. They were all there: Kako Pino, Bido Sherifi's wife, Ilir's mother, Lady Majnur (still holding her nose), Nazo and her pretty daughter-in-law. Only Xhexho, who had disappeared once again, was missing. Çeço Kaili still wouldn't come. Aqif Kashahu now sent only his sons, at whom Bido Sherifi stared in terror, God knows why. Aqif himself, his deaf mother, his wife and his daughter stayed home.

The snow muffled the rumble of the planes and the roar of artillery. The sound of the old anti-aircraft gun was still different from the others. But by now no one expected it to do any good. It was like an old blind man teased by kids, who responds by throwing stones that never hit their mark.

The English planes paid us regular visits every day. They would loom in the sky almost to a schedule, and people seemed to get used to the bombings as a disagreeable part of a daily routine. "See you tomorrow at the coffee house, right after the bombing." "I'll be up at dawn tomorrow; that way I think I'll have the house cleaned before the bombing." "Come on, let's go down to the cellar, it's almost time."

But no one suspected that the cellar's days were numbered. *That its time had passed.*

That judgment was uttered by a man who came down the stairs wearing a black cape over his shoulders.

"Who's that?"

"What does that man want?"

"Make way for your visitor. He's a foreign engineer. He wants to check the shelter."

"An engineer?"

The interpreter threaded a path through the blankets and mattresses where the sick people and pregnant women were lying. The foreigner in the black cape followed. He asked for a chair.

"Good God, where did that man come from?"

"Don't look at him like that."

"What's he going to do with that knife? Lord have mercy!"

The man in the black cape stood on the chair they had brought him. He took out of his tool-bag a knife with a finer point and a sturdy hammer. He gave his bag to the interpreter, then raised his right arm and hit the ceiling with the hammer in several places. Then he handed the hammer to the interpreter, and took one of the knives. His arm shot up and with a jab, almost taking it by surprise, he dug the knife into the ceiling. We all held our breath. The man pulled the knife out slowly. Bits of rubble fell to the floor with a clatter. The tip of the knife had turned slightly white. He got down from the chair, moved a little farther over, got up again, and did the same thing again, this time with both knives. Now both blades were white with plaster. The foreign engineer got down off the chair and said a few words to the interpreter.

In a loud, mechanical voice, the interpreter translated, "This cellar is unsuitable for use as a shelter. Whose house is this?"

My father came forward.

"Your cellar is inadequate as a shelter," he repeated to my father with the same indifference, looking past him at the wall as if he was reading off it.

My father shrugged.

The foreigner said something else.

"The engineer says the cellar has to be evacuated immediately. It would be dangerous to stay here."

No one said a word. The engineer's knives had slashed not only the walls but everyone's flesh too; you could tell by the painful way their wrinkles tightened and contracted.

The man in the black cape strode towards the exit. His cape billowed out behind him as he went up the steps, cutting off for a moment the feeble light that streamed in from outside, then letting it in again.

"My God," said a neighbour of ours who suffered from rheumatism. "Where are we supposed to go now?"

Some of the women began to wail.

"Where are they going to put us now?"

"Enough," Bido Sherifi cried. "We'll find another shelter somewhere. Stop crying."

"It's not the end of the world."

"We'll find a place. There has to be another place."

"They say they're going to open the citadel to the public."

"The citadel?"

"Why not? It's possible. Come on, let's get the blankets together," Bido Sherifi said to his wife.

One by one people started to go. The cellar was emptying. By afternoon the last to leave, the sick and the pregnant women, were gone. The door creaked in complaint. We were left alone.

All was silence. I went upstairs. You could hear worms gnawing at the wood. So quiet you could hear a worm munching . . . I listened for a long time to a monotonous crackling whose source I couldn't locate. The time of the worms has come, I thought.

I went downstairs. There was no one in the hallway. The lamp was there, and the candle too, its black wick bowing its head sadly. I lit it and, holding it gingerly, started down the stairs to the cellar. I could feel the smell of people drifting up. The candle's flickering light swept over the white walls. On the ceiling I could see the small wounds left by the knife of the man in the black cape.

The engineer in black was all we talked about during that time. He showed up everywhere, and everywhere he declared cellars unsuitable as shelters. Just as he had done at our place, he would start by asking for a chair and then, with a quick, almost sly thrust of his arm, he would stab old cellars to death. One hundred and sixty-three cellars large and small were cleared out in just four days. On the fifth day, before heading back to Tirana, the engineer got roaring drunk on the local raki and, getting into his car, said that he was sorry to be leaving behind a city doomed to destruction but that it wasn't his fault, he had done all he could, the days of his visit had been terribly painful for him too, but in the end no one could fight fate. There comes a time, he said, when not only cities but even kingdoms and empires must perish.

As if to bear out the engineer's words, the English bombing suddenly intensified. Forty-nine people were killed in four days. In the town hall the council met in continuous session to decide whether to open the citadel to the public. They had been deliberating for three days when the inhabitants of Lower Dunavat breached the citadel's western gate without waiting for the council's decision. On the same day the people of the market district forced the eastern gate.

That day, from morning to evening, there was a long migration to the citadel.

Doors slammed shut in our street all night.

"You going too?"

"Yes. Are you?"

"We'll decide later this evening."

"There may not be enough room for everyone."

"I think it'll be all right. The cellars under the citadel are huge."

Kako Pino came over for a consultation.

"What are we going to do? It's the end of the world."

"We'll see tomorrow," my father said.

Bido Sherifi came in.

"Tomorrow," my father repeated. "Go to Mane Voco's," he told me, "and ask them what they mean to do."

I ran into Mane Voco in the street. He was on his way to our house.

A little later Nazo and her daughter-in-law knocked at our door.

"So, tomorrow?"

"Yes, tomorrow before dawn."

It was one of the happiest evenings of my life. People knocked at the door endlessly. No one dreamt of going to sleep. We wrapped things in big bundles and carried them down into the cellar to protect them from fire. Bido Sherifi, Nazo, Kako Pino and Mane Voco also brought bundles over. The cellar had become useful again.

"Go to bed," Grandmother told me two or three times.

I just could not. Tomorrow we were going to the citadel. We would say good-bye to the steps, doors and windows of our house, leave the familiar words behind and enter the unknown. Everything there would be magical, terrifying and extraordinary. It was the very place where Macbeth lived.

Morning came, cold and dull. A light rain was falling. There was a knock at the door.

"Well, are you ready?" Bido Sherifi called from the street.

"Ready," my father answered.

"Come here, let me kiss you," Grandmother said. I stood there dumbfounded.

"Why, aren't you coming with us?"

She stroked my head.

"No, I'm staying here."

"No! No!"

"Be quiet!" my father told me.

"Hush, my darling. Nothing will happen to me."

"No! No!"

Another knock.

"Hurry up," my father said, "they're waiting for us."

"Why are we leaving Grandmother all alone here?" I cried out reproachfully.

"She won't come," my father said. "I tried all night to convince her, but she won't budge." Then, turning to Grandmother: "Look, for the last time, come with us. Please."

"I won't leave the house all on its own," she said calmly. "This is where I've spent my life, and this is where I want to die."

Another knock.

"Bless you all," said Grandmother, kissing each of us in turn.

The door closed behind us and we were in the street. It was still drizzling. We set off. Others joined our group along the way. You could barely see the citadel walls through the mist. A line of people several hundred metres long stretched out from the western gate. Carrying bundles, blankets, trunks, suitcases, books, pots, chairs, carpets, wash-basins, pitchers, cradles, grinders and bowls, they moved forward slowly, stopped, waited a long time, and moved again. It was a long way to the gate. Everything was soaked by the rain. People coughed, stood on tiptoe to see what was going on at the head of the queue, asked, "Why have they stopped moving?" and coughed some more.

By noon, we were finally getting close to the guard post. The ancient walls, streaming with rain, rose up on either side. The gate was high but narrow. When we went through (by now my joy had vanished), we found ourselves in total darkness. There was a terrifying echo of footsteps. The children began to scream in terror. We couldn't see a thing. We were feeling our way along blindly. Someone screamed. Suddenly, somewhere up ahead of us, we saw a jagged piece of sky. We walked in that direction. The crack widened overhead until we felt raindrops on our heads again.

"This way! Come this way!" someone yelled frantically.

We climbed a few stairs, then crossed a relatively flat area and entered an arched tunnel that led to a small platform.

"This way!"

We were led into another tunnel that was completely dark. The floor was on a sharp incline, and it was hard to stay upright. Then another piece of sky cut into the blackness. This time we came out onto a sort of open esplanade, bounded on either side by battlements. Right in front of us, rising to a great height as if it were trying to take a bite out of the sky, loomed the prison.

"This way!"

We crossed the square and went into another vaulted tunnel. I reckoned we must now be right under the prison. A muffled commotion came from somewhere up ahead of us.

At last we came upon a strange sight: under the majestic,

high-vaulted ceiling dripping with water, amidst the bundles and blankets, cradles and countless random items, sat thousands of people, immobile or shifting about, silent or noisy, coughing, sneezing, crying.

For a long time we wandered among the throng and the piles of luggage, looking for a place to settle down. Our ears rang with the amplified noise bouncing two and three times off the high arches. There was no empty space anywhere. Someone advised us to look in the second gallery, and pointed the way. We went. It was just as crowded as the one before. Finally Mane Voco, who was leading our group, found a narrow strip that seemed to have remained unoccupied because of the icy draught that blew in through a crack in the wall. We put our things down and started to spread out our mats and thick woollen blankets. You could see part of the city through the chink in the wall. It was way below us, far below, sunk in its grey depths, majestic and scornful.

"Peanuts! Peanuts!"

A youngster was actually selling peanuts. Then we saw other street peddlers snaking through the crowd, crying "Hashure! Hot saleep!" or "Cigarettes!" News vendors were there too.

The first night in the citadel was cold and restless. The sound of thousands of coughs echoed off the great stone arches. Blankets rustled, cradles creaked, everything groaned, scratched or bumped around. All night you could hear footsteps nearby. We were huddled together. Water trickled down on us.

Around midnight I woke up. A hoarse voice droned: "Got to get out. We're in a trap here . . . One of these nights they'll lock the doors and slaughter us all like sheep. Got to get out. No matter what, before it's too late . . . Anyway, it's a citadel . . . Medieval . . . You understand? . . . Darkness, like in the year 1,000. Nothing has changed. It just seems that way, sure . . . but in fact it's not any easier."

"Who's talking such drivel?" Bido Sherifi's sleepy wife asked.

"Begone, Satan," murmured Kako Pino.

The voice fell silent.

Towards dawn there was heavy bombing.

It was a gloomy morning, the light barely squeezing in through the narrow loopholes and chinks in the wall. The citadel began to come to life around seven o'clock. People were wandering through the tunnels and passageways once again, running into more and more acquaintances. Everyone was upset about the whole city's waking up under one roof. Families were encamped alongside one another with no respect for rank or order. Boundaries and distances between neighbourhoods and houses had been rudely overturned; spatial orientation was confused. This common roof housed people who had seemed irreconcilable: Karllashis and Angonis, Muslims and Christians, nuns and prostitutes, the scions of great families, street cleaners and gypsies.

Some families, however, had not taken refuge in the citadel. For the most part, they were families in some kind of disgrace or which had something to hide. None of the old crones had come either.

On the second day in the citadel, back in the first gallery, we ran into Grandfather and some of our cousins among their retinue of gypsies. Babazoti was lying on his chaise longue,

ISMAIL KADARE

which he had brought along with him. He was reading a
Turkish book, ignoring the crowds milling around him. Suzana
was nowhere in sight.

"What does this 'medieval' mean?" Ilir asked me.

"I don't know. Did you hear that madman in the middle
of the night too?"

"Yes."

"Let's ask Javer."

Isa and Javer disappeared from time to time. We went
and found them.

"'Medieval,'" Javer said, "refers to the Middle Ages, the
bleakest period in history. The story of that Macbeth you read
is set in that age."

Certain people were associating the citadel with the
Middle Ages more and more. The fortress was indeed very
old. It had given birth to the city, and our houses resembled
the citadel the way children look like their mothers. Over the
centuries, the city had grown up a lot. Although the fortress
was in good condition, no one ever thought that one day it
would have the strength to take its offspring, the city, under
its protection. That was a terrifying return to the past. It was
like someone going back into the womb. Now that it had
happened, we all wondered what would be next. Having
accepted the citadel's services, we now had to suffer the conse-
quences. There might be epidemics as there were in the Middle
Ages. Age-old crimes might come back. Xivo Gavo's chronicle was full of murders and epidemics.

One morning — it was our fifth day in the citadel —
Ilir and I were wandering aimlessly through the human jumble.
We had already been tempted more than once to leave the

tunnels and explore other parts of the fortress, but fear had stopped us. The place was said to be full of mysterious crannies, catacombs and labyrinths you could never find your way out of. Near certain dark passageways, we had noticed people, from a distance, who seemed to be paying no attention to us but who, on closer inspection, turned out to be guards.

Roaming through the first gallery, we suddenly caught a few sentence fragments in the midst of the general commotion. Two tall, pale, middle-aged men wearing scarves around their necks were talking. Their voices were strangely monotonous. We forgot everything and fell in quietly behind them. We were captivated. The chains of their words shackled our arms and legs.

"Did the edict with the death sentence come on Monday?"

"No, it was already here on Saturday. Monday was the execution. The palace guard took the head away in a sack. They threw the rest of the body into the chasm from the eastern tower. The officer left for the capital that night."

"Had he been poisoned when they cut off his head?"

"No, he was just drunk. They put the head in the Nook of Shame in Istanbul, according to custom."

"I've seen that nook."

"They kept the head there for eleven days, and took it out only to replace it with the head of Kara Razi. You know the rules say that there must be only one head in the nook at a time."

They kept talking. We were following behind. We had left the tunnel and started across the esplanade. It was raining. Everything was wet and deserted. They walked into a narrow passage, went down some stone steps, up some other steps and into an abandoned gallery. We shivered like freezing puppies.

The gallery had a low ceiling, and the echo of our steps came from overhead instead of underfoot. Their words began to twist; they swelled and stretched, endlessly elongated. We couldn't understand a thing. That lasted until we reached the end of the gallery. We finally came to a large pit with a domed ceiling. There they turned and noticed us. They stared at us for a long time with their grey eyes. We couldn't stop shivering. Then they looked away, and one of them pointed to some rusty irons hanging from the wall.

"This is where they kept Gur Çerçizi. Chained to those shackles right there. Third from the right. They kept him chained up long after he was dead. When they took the body away, it was half-eaten by rats."

"What about Karafili? They were imprisoned together, weren't they?"

"Yes, Karafili was chained up over there, the fifth set. He lived until the sultan's edict came pardoning him. They took him up to a platform with no parapet at the top of the citadel and everyone thought he would be delirious with joy. When he began walking towards the edge of the wall, someone said he seemed blind, but no one paid attention. He walked to the rampart and when he got to the edge everyone expected him to stop and look down at the beautiful view, make some short statement or just thank the sultan for pardoning him. But instead he took another step and dropped off the cliff. It was only then that everyone realised that he really had lost his sight."

Now we were going up some stairs. The stones were slippery.

"Hurshid Pasha's head rolled down these very steps. The right eye was crushed when it fell and the officer who brought the head to the capital was punished. They accused him of not having taken proper care of it during the trip and of not sprinkling it with salt as the rules require."

"If I'm not mistaken, the rule about the salt was instituted by Bugrahan, the chief physician, after suspicion arose about the head of Timurtash. Isn't that right?"

"No, the suspicions were about the head of Velldrem. It had changed so much after decapitation that there were those who doubted that it was really his. That was when they instituted the rules."

They went on chatting about heads for a long time. Absolutely spellbound, we followed them. Their necks were carefully wrapped in their shawls. For a minute it seemed to me that those black shawls were only meant to hold on their heads (long since cut off), to prevent them from rolling to the ground.

I began to feel sick. They were going upstairs now. The air was cooler. We came out into the open.

"Peanuts! Peanuts!"

At last we were safe. We ran like madmen through the packed gallery, looking for our families.

"Where were you? Why are you so pale?" our mothers asked almost simultaneously. "Why are you shaking like that?"

"We're cold."

Mamma wrapped us in a big wool blanket. Ilir's mother gave us each some bread and marmalade. It was nice and warm there, among the living. Some women had come to visit. My father and Bido Sherifi were talking, looking serious. Nazo's daughter-in-law, chin resting in her hand, stared sadly. Kako Pino was fidgeting with the little yellow bag where she kept her equipment. There would always be weddings, always and everywhere, now and till the end of time, she had replied, when on the first day of the move to the citadel someone had asked why she was taking her bag along. Nazo's daughter-in-law sighed. Yes, life was nice among living people.

Ilir and I didn't budge from that spot for the rest of the afternoon and the next day. We sat listening to what the women who came to see our mothers had to say. We were scared to death of running into the two strangers with the black scarves around their necks. We had decided that if we ever encountered them in the crowd, we would plug up our ears as fast as we could so we wouldn't hear anything they said. Otherwise, if we let their words get into our ears, we would be shackled by them once more and would not be able to resist falling in step behind the men.

That night there was heavy bombing. I kept thinking of Grandmother. Her now solitary footsteps must be echoing through the big house. Up and down the steps. Sighs of wood and old age, and the curse of death she hurled at nations, governments and their planes.

Ilir and I sat in a corner drifting off to sleep when suddenly — like a snake that slithers under your feet before you even see it — the word "arrest" rang out. Necks craned, eyes narrowed, boots marched towards us. Trak-truk, trak-truk. "Under arrest." Trak-truk. An Italian carabiniere pulled some handcuffs from his pocket. A tall man watched the handcuffs being put on him.

"Look, they're locking those things on him with a key," Ilir said to me.

"I saw."

A woman, apparently the arrested man's wife, let out a short, sharp scream.

"Don't worry," her husband said.

One of the carabinieri took him by the elbow and the little group moved off.

"Dirty fascists," someone muttered.

The people who had gathered to watch now dispersed in silence. At noon there was more heavy bombing.

The next day I saw a face I thought I recognised among the people filing past endlessly. He was staring at me. I had seen that fair hair and those troubled eyes somewhere before. At last it came to me. This was the boy who had kissed Aqif Kashahu's daughter in our cellar during the bombing.

After hanging around us for a while, he motioned to me. I shrugged. He gestured for me to follow him. He seemed not to want to come over. I got up and followed him. We went out onto the wide esplanade. It was chilly.

"What's your name?" the boy asked me.

I told him. We had stopped near a battlement, and the icy wind cut your face like a knife. The city lay in the chasm below.

"Do you recognise me?" he asked.

"Yes," I said.

"OK then. It was right in your cellar. Do you know what happened?" He grabbed me sharply by the shoulders. "Yes or no, say something! Do you know or not?"

"I know," I told him.

The boy who had kissed Aqif Kashahu's daughter took a deep breath.

"All right, have you seen her since . . . ?"

"No."

He clamped his jaw tight.

"In this city love is forbidden," he said in a lower voice. "You'll find out some day, when you grow up."

(. . . garita!)

He kept kicking the rampart with the tip of his shoe.

"Listen," he said. "I'm afraid they may have killed her. What do you think?"

I shrugged.

"In this city there are two ways to get rid of pregnant girls: suffocate them in a *juk* or drown them in a well. What do you think?"

I shrugged again. It was getting even colder.

"So you haven't seen her anywhere in the neighbourhood?"

"Nowhere."

"No one has seen her?"

"No one."

"Are there many wells in your neighbourhood?"

"A few."

He started biting his nails.

"If only I could find her body," he said dully.

The wind was blowing. I was freezing.

"I'll look for her everywhere," he added.

He had unusually long fingers. He looked out at the grey cliffs. The city's numberless roofs were barely visible in the fog.

"If I can't find her, I'll go to hell to look for her."

I wanted to ask him what he meant by that, but I was afraid.

Without another word he walked off quickly across the esplanade.

They were flying slowly, their wings outspread, and for a moment I thought they were going to land on the abandoned airfield, but they turned abruptly and headed for the city. Their wings flashed in the sun with menace. Now they were almost overhead, just at the altitude from which they usually started their dive-bombing. One last manoeuvre and they swooped down on the city one after another, almost vertically.

It was spring now. From the window two flights up, I was watching the storks fly back. Circling the tops of minarets and the tall chimneys, they looked for their old nests, and the ellipses they traced in the sky clearly showed just how sad and dismayed they were to find their nests damaged or destroyed by the impact of the bombs and by the wind and rain of the past winter. As I watched them, I was thinking that storks could never imagine what could happen to a city in the winter, while they were away.

XII

It was Sunday. From below came the noise of the pick swung by a neighbour who had been working for two weeks on a modern air-raid shelter like the one Lady Majnur had just had built. The bombing had stopped when spring began. We had been back in our homes for some time. The Karllashis and Angonis were the first to build modern shelters and leave the citadel. Next to leave were the nuns and prostitutes, whose shelters had been taken care of by the army. Then the people who had the money to build their own modern shelters went home. But most of us left the citadel only after the English bombing had eased. The first thing that struck me when we went home was that the tin sign saying "shelter for 90 persons" was gone. Someone must have taken it down while we were away, and the wall now had a light rectangular mark that gave me an empty feeling in my heart every time I looked at it.

Our neighbour's pickaxe continued its regular thud. Sunday had spread out all over the city. It looked as if the sun had smacked into the earth and broken into pieces, and chunks of wet light were scattered everywhere — in the streets, on the windowpanes, on puddles and roofs. I remembered a day long ago when Grandmother had scaled a big fish. Her forearms were splattered with shiny scales. It was as if she was a Sunday all over. When my father got angry, he was a Tuesday.

I could hear the voices of Grandmother and Aunt Xhemo coming from the other room. They were still talking about the same thing. The neighbourhood women who had been coming by all morning, detailing ever more astounding pieces of news, had gone home to prepare lunch, but Grandmother and Aunt Xhemo went back to the conversation they had been having the previous Sunday. It seemed to me that all their chatting derived from prior conversations, which were themselves the sequels of even older discussions going back to ancient times. I had also noticed that some topics of current interest were never broached directly. They would circle round the old ladies like buzzing flies, but could not cross the barrier of their indifference. At best, a topic of that kind would take two or three weeks to gain admittance to the conversation, but most never achieved such a privilege.

All morning, the local women had made a whole series of guesses about a very recent event. My mother, as she brought Grandma and Aunt Xhemo their coffee, had asked them two or three times: "Have you heard the latest?" Obstinate as they were, they pretended not to hear, and they carried on elaborating a conversation that had been begun long ago, in the first year of the monarchy, or perhaps even further back, in the year 1901. Sitting beside them, I waited in vain for the expression of some opinion on the latest news. It was one of the few occasions when I felt angry with the old ladies. Stubborn as mules! I muttered to myself. Did they not grasp that the issue ought to make them prick up their ears, or were they dragging things out just to heighten the expectation that they would have something to say?

What had happened was deeply disturbing to me. Someone had gone into our cistern the night before. Fresh footprints were everywhere. Whoever it was had not even replaced the cover, and ashes had been found in a bucket that still smelled of kerosene. Apparently the intruder had used it as a torch to light the inside of the cistern.

For some time now there had been rumours that someone, or rather, some ghost, had been going down into the neighbourhood wells at night. *Are there many wells in your neighbourhood . . . ?* At first, the old ladies thought it was the ghost of someone called Xuano, who had been murdered in a dispute over property and was now seeking the gold he had hidden. But Aqif Kashahu's deaf mother, who never slept at night, swore that with her own eyes she had seen the man coming out of their well at daybreak. *If I can't find her, I'll go to hell to look for her . . .* She had even spoken to him and, strangest of all, by her own account, she had seen his lips move in reply, but as she was deaf she hadn't understood any of what was said.

Was it really him?

The roofs seemed dazed by the light. I walked over to the pile of bedding. The mattresses, blankets, pillows and lace-edged sheets — that whole soft white heap that was called *juk* — lay silent as a snare. *In this city there are two ways to get rid of pregnant girls: suffocate them in a juk or drown them in a well.*

Was it really him?

Two or three times I went up to the mirror and, after making it go misty with my breath, put my lips on its ice-cold surface. The shape of my kiss remained clear. It was a cold, joyless kiss, redolent with death.

I tried to summon up the face of the boy as I had seen him the other day, up in the fortress. I tried especially hard to remember his lips, which had caught my eye that day more than anything else about his face. They were special lips: lips that had already kissed.

The days went by with nothing to report. A person was looking for the body of another, whom he had once kissed. That was happening somewhere deep down, under the ground. Up above, everything was as before. The days were heavy and shapeless. All identical. Soon they would lose their one remaining distinction, the names that sheltered them like snail shells: Monday, Wednesday, Thursday.

Nothing happening. Wednesday and Thursday went by. Then Frisatsunday. The days stuck to each other like lumps of sticky dough. Finally, on Tuesday, something happened: after the rain, a little rainbow came out. In our city, spring came from the sky, not from the soil, which was ruled by stone that knows no seasons. The coming of spring could be glimpsed in the thinning of clouds, the appearance of birds, and the occasional rainbow. This one rose up inside the city itself. Strangely, one end of it rested on the brothel, the other on Aunt Xhemo's house, which was nonetheless considered one of the most respectable houses in town.

"Kako Pino, go out and look," Bido Sherifi's wife called out.

"It's the end of the world," Kako Pino said. "Selfixhe, come and look!"

Grandmother looked and shook her head.

After the rainbow nothing happened for a whole week. Then one day Ilir said to me, "Isa and Javer are going to do something."

"What?"

"I don't know. But I heard Javer saying: 'We have to break the peace and quiet of this petty-bor . . . petty-boar . . .' I can't remember the word."

"Could they have meant to say pretty-boring?"

"No, it definitely wasn't that."

"I don't believe it," I said.

"Why not?"

"Remember their death list? How come they never did anyone in?"

"Who knows? There might have been a good reason."

"They won't do anything now either."

"I'm sure they will."

"Yiorgos Poulos changed his name back to Giorgio Pulo. Why don't they shoot him?"

"Want to bet they'll do something this time?"

"OK."

"I'll bet France and two Switzerlands against Madagascar."

"It's a deal."

Three days later, I lost France and two Switzerlands. Something serious happened all right: the town hall burned down. Very early in the morning we heard gunfire, then, coming from the street, people shouting: "The town hall is burning! The town hall is burning!" Shutters flew open.

Heads, hands and arms stretched out as if they wanted to catch the news while it was still in the air. And it was true, the town hall was really going up in flames. Thick smoke like a herd of black horses was rising over the massive building and being blown around by the wind. Tongues of fire glowed red here and there against the black. Footsteps rang through the streets, then a hoarse voice shouted, "The title deeds are burning!"

"The deeds?" a woman asked from her window.

The hoarse voice kept shouting, "Citizens, come out, the town hall and the *deeds* are burning!"

"What are *deeds*?" I whispered.

No one answered.

The sound of footsteps in the street turned to thunder. I took advantage of the confusion to slip out. Mane Voco's house was nearby. Ilir opened the door.

"Did you bring France and two Switzerlands?" he asked as I came in.

"Don't worry. I'll give them to you. But wait a minute. What's going on?"

"It burned down. It's gone."

"Was it them?"

"Of course. Who else?"

"Where are they?"

"In their room. Pretending to be surprised, to know nothing about it."

"What are deeds?"

"I don't know."

"Come in and close the door!" Ilir's mother shouted from upstairs.

We went upstairs. Ilir knocked on his brother's door.

"Can we come in for a minute?" he asked.

We went in, first Ilir, then me.

Isa and Javer were both there. They were standing at the window watching the fire. They said something to each other in a foreign language.

"Strange," Javer commented. "I wonder who started the fire? What are they saying over at your place?" he asked, turning to me.

"Yes, very strange all right," Isa agreed.

"I was having a nice dream when the shots woke me up," said Javer.

"Me too," said Isa. "I was dreaming about flowers."

There were shouts from the street.

"What are deeds?" This time it was Ilir who asked the question.

"Ah yes, deeds," Javer said. "Can you hear them weeping and wailing over their precious deeds? Deeds are documents saying who is the owner of things like houses, yards and land. Understand?"

It was hard to follow. They both tried to explain it to us.

"All the information about property is written down in the deeds: where it lies, who inherits it from one generation to the next, things like that. Have you got that into your thick skulls? Everything is written down — the cistern, the fig tree in the back, the mortgage your father took out, and even you . . ."

Out in the streets, the shouts were getting louder and louder.

"Listen to them bleating," said Isa. "The monster of private property has been wounded."

A shrill cry rose above the general clamour.

"Lady Majnur," said Javer, leaning out to hear better.

Lady Majnur had run into the street without her hat. The wisps of grey hair that poked out from under her black headscarf made a terrifying sight. Her shouts were punctuated by fragments of words and sprays of spit.

"The rabble! . . . It's the debtors who set fire to the title deeds! . . . Communists! . . . Criminals! . . ."

"Scream, you old witch! Scream your head off, you old whore!" Javer snarled.

I plastered my face to the windowpane and looked out at the teeming street. Now and again the pane misted over. The land and houses, now they were free of the weight of their deeds, began to shift, wander and come apart. The walls seemed to part from their footings, and the age-old ties that had held them in place for so long seemed to have come asunder. As they drifted about, the great stone houses sometimes came dangerously close to each other. They could easily collide and destroy themselves, as they did in earthquakes.

"They're burning, they're burning!"

Only the streets, which belonged to everyone, tried to keep their heads in the uproar.

The chaos went on for a while. Smoke now rose more languidly from the burned-out building. The windows, from which flames had been leaping furiously only a short while before, had now begun to go dark.

"The Reichstag went up in flames as well," said Javer, pointing to a place on the globe.

"Who burned it?" Ilir asked.

"Who? Arsonists, obviously," Javer said.

"Every city in this world has a building that should be burned," Isa said.

Javer smiled. A moment later he gave such a yawn he could have dislocated his jaw. He had rings under his eyes. Isa was yawning a lot too. Neither tried to hide the fact that they hadn't had a wink of sleep. I felt sure that if you got up close to them, they would smell of kerosene.

Outside, the streets had almost settled down. I went out.

That night, someone was arrested in our street. There were loud knocks at someone's door, knocks that didn't sound like the usual ones, and they woke up half the neighbourhood.

"Who did they take away?" Grandmother asked as she opened the street-side shutters.

"We don't know yet," someone whispered. "But I think it was one of Mezini's sons."

The next day we found out that there had been arrests all over the city. A big notice was posted in the town square offering a reward of forty thousand leks for information leading to the identification of the arsonist.

On the third night, the police arrested a stranger. They had followed him for a while before making the arrest. The stranger walked as if dazed, clutching a bottle of kerosene (you could smell it from far off) and carrying a rope coiled over his shoulder. It was midnight. There was no doubt he was the arsonist. A box of matches and a little pouch of ashes were found in his pockets.

The next day people said that the boy who had kissed

Aqif Kashahu's daughter had been caught. Despite the calamities that had befallen it all last winter ("May we never live to see another winter like that," the old women said), the city had not forgotten the fair-haired boy. Despite themselves, Grandma and Aunt Xhemo were finally obliged to allude to the event during their conversation, though they only touched on it briefly. Every one else was clucking and chortling with indignation.

"Did you hear what the boy who kissed Aqif Kashahu's daughter told the magistrate?"

"What? He burned down the town hall?"

"No, he did not. The kerosene and ashes he was carrying when he was arrested were for something completely different."

"Really?"

"He was going down into wells at night looking for the girl."

"Down into wells at night? What people will do for love!"

"According to the boy, her own family killed her."

"Today around noon the magistrate went to the Kashahus' and asked to talk to the girl. She wasn't in. The boy maintains she's been murdered."

"Now that you mention it, I confess I've not seen her either, since the *kiss*."

"Like I said. You're not the only one. Nobody's set eyes on her."

"You're right! Go on!"

"Now, where was I? Oh yes. Aqif Kashahu said that he'd sent his daughter off to visit some distant cousins."

"Oh, distant cousins . . ."

"You don't look well," Grandmother said to me. "Go spend a few days at Babazoti's."

I had been waiting for that.

FRAGMENT OF A CHRONICLE

now clear that a group of terrorists is currently operating in the city. When the police arrested the young man with the kerosene and the rope in the middle of the night, everyone thought that the Nero of our city had been caught at last. But it turned out he was not Nero but Orpheus, seeking his Eurydice in the wells of our courtyards. Trial. Executive measures. Property. All suits relating to property are suspended because of the burning of the land registry. Today Jur Qosja published an announcement in the newspaper denying the rumour that he had been to Salonica to see doctors about his lack of facial hair. "I went to buy raisins, as I do every year," he told the newspaper. Cinema. Tomorrow: *Grand Hotel*, starring the famous actress Greta Garbo. I hereby prohibit all traffic between nine at night and four in the morning, except for midwives. City Commandant Bruno Arcivocale. Price of bread.

XIII

As in other years, I found that the landscape around Grandfather's house had changed. At first glance things looked the same, but closer inspection revealed that certain paths were gone and others were slowly dying, while still others, new and frail but determined, were springing up amid the dust and grass.

As always, Babazoti was lying on his chaise longue, reading. Grandma was hanging the laundry out to dry. White sheets billowed in the fresh breeze. Bushes had sprouted everywhere. Taking advantage of the neglect caused by the spring bombing, they had launched a furious attack on the house.

The flapping and flailing of the sheets on the clothesline as they resisted the wind's onslaught made a most peaceful sight. It has to be said that the wind was far from vicious that day, and was only attacking the sheets in a playful way.

The wind blew steadily from the same direction. Maybe it would bring Suzana.

Grandma finished hanging out the sheets.

"So, how are your mother and father? And Selfixhe?" she asked, clipping on the last peg.

"Everyone's fine."

Alongside the flapping of sheets I could make out the sound of something else.

"You look a little distracted," Grandma said. "No wonder too, with all those bombs and planes."

The alert came from a young and pretty siren . . . There she was, flying through the air. Her white wings sparkled in the sunlight. She appeared for a moment in the sky between the clouds, then was gone again.

I went outside the yard. And there she was, with her head leaning slightly to one side, dressed in a light grey skirt the colour of aluminium.

"Suzana!"

She turned round.

"Oh, you're back."

"Yes."

She had grown.

"Since when?"

"Today."

Her legs were even longer and shapelier.

"Where did you go during the bombing?" I asked her.

"There, in that cave over there."

"We went to the citadel. I even went looking for you once."

"Really? I thought you wouldn't even remember me."

"No, I haven't forgotten you."

She turned her head and adjusted a hairpin.

"Big deal! You didn't forget me!" she said sharply and then ran off.

I saw the aluminium-grey dress flash once among the trees along the road to her house. Then when she got near the cliff edge, she branched off. By the badshade tree she slackened her pace, before turning round and coming back to me.

"Well, will you tell me things?" she asked, almost sternly.

"Sure, I'll tell you things."

Her eyes shone with pleasure.

"Many things?"

"A lot, yes."

"Well, go ahead. Come on, start," she said.

We sat down on the grass by the side of the road and I started telling her things. It wasn't easy. I had so much to say that it got all jumbled up in my head. She was listening very attentively, her eyes open wide, frowning as though in pain every time I got in a muddle or put things in the wrong order or didn't give them the importance she thought they deserved. Sometimes I got carried away by my story and boldly altered the facts. When I told her about the Englishman's arm, for example, I said that Aqif Kashahu kept biting it in rage and that the crowd cheered every time he did. She listened carefully to everything, but when I started telling her how a man called Macbeth had invited someone to dinner whose name I couldn't remember any more and how he had cut his guest's head off, but then it turned out he didn't know the rules about sprinkling salt on a severed head, she put her hand over my mouth and pleaded: "Tell me about something less gruesome, OK?"

So I told her about Lady Majnur screaming in the streets the day the town hall burned down, and about Vasiliqia, and about how when Grandmother heard that Vasiliqia had come she said she wished she had died the winter before. I was

telling her about Aunt Xhemo's last visit and the defeat of
the Greeks when I heard my elder aunt calling me for lunch.

They were all at table already. The signs of a quarrel
were obvious. My younger aunt was pouting.

"I don't want to see that good for nothing around here
any more, you hear?" Grandma said, throwing some food on
a plate.

"He's a friend, he lends me books," my younger aunt
answered stubbornly.

"Books! You should be ashamed. Love stories to corrupt
your mind."

"They're not love stories, they're about politics."

"So much the worse. One of these days you'll have the
carabinieri over here."

"That's enough now," said Babazoti.

It was a short truce.

"You're a big girl now," Grandma started up again. "You
don't see your girlfriends neglecting their embroidery. One of
these days you'll take a husband."

My younger aunt stuck her tongue out, as she always did
at the mention of marriage.

The next day I saw Suzana again. She seemed pensive.

"What did the Englishman's ring look like?" she asked.

"Very pretty. It sparkled in the sun."

"Who do you think gave it to him?"

I shrugged.

"How should I know?"

Suzana stared at me so hard that it seemed she was trying
to find another pair of eyes behind mine.

"Maybe his fiancée," she said.

"Maybe."

Suzana took me by the arm.

"Listen," she whispered into my ear. "Of all the things you told me, what sticks in my mind the most is what happened to Aqif Kashahu's daughter. Will you tell it to me again?"

I nodded.

"Only this time, try to remember everything."

I thought for a moment.

"Take your time," she said. "Try to remember."

I frowned to make her think I was trying hard to recall the slightest details, but in fact completely unrelated pieces of events had pushed their way into my mind.

"Now tell the story," she said.

She was all ears. Her eyes, her hair, her thin arms, everything about her was frozen as she listened.

When I finished, she took a deep breath.

"What strange things happen in this world," she said.

"One of my friends has a little world made of papier mâché," I told her. "You can spin it with your finger."

She wasn't listening any more. Her mind was elsewhere.

"Do you want to go to the cave?" she asked.

I didn't really feel like it. I was pretty sick of cellars and damp places, but I didn't want to spoil her fun.

It was cool in the cave. We sat down on two big rocks and didn't say a word.

Suddenly she said, "Let's pretend the planes are coming and dropping their bombs. Can you hear? There's a whole lot of them. The siren is wailing. Bombs are falling right next to us. When do the lights go out?"

"Now."

She reached out and put her arms around my neck. Her soft cheek pressed against mine.

"Like this?" she asked.

"Yes."

Her arms were as cold as aluminium. There was a good smell of soap from her neck.

"Someone has put the light back on," she said in a little while. "They'll see us."

I held my neck very stiff. Suzana quickly let go of me.

"Now they're dragging me by the hair. Can you see? What are you going to do?"

"I'll go down to hell," I said, putting on a booming voice. She burst out laughing.

We played that same little game a few more times that day and the next. I got to like sitting motionless while she wrapped her long arms around my neck. Her neck always had that nice smell of soap. A sensation I'd never had before made me feel alternately unbearably heavy and intoxicated, as if I was flying.

I was expecting her to ask me again if I knew any rude words. But she said nothing and kept her eyes half-shut. Apparently that was how she could best meditate on what had happened to Aqif Kashahu's daughter.

I was tempted to say, don't think any more about that girl, she's probably dead, but I was afraid of scaring Suzana. One of the gypsies who lived in the shed told me that all girls have the black triangle I'd seen on Margarita. For me, that was an indisputable sign that they would end up in dishonour.

One day (here they had no Thursdays or Tuesdays like in our neighbourhood, just mornings, afternoons and nights) we were sitting and hugging, counting the bombs that were falling more and more furiously, when a shadow appeared at the entrance to the cave. I saw it first, but there was nothing I could do.

"Suzana!" her mother called.

Suzana jerked her arms off my neck and sat there petrified. The woman whose face we couldn't see in the darkness with the sunlight behind her came closer.

"So this is where you've been hiding all day," she said quietly but sternly. (Aqif Kashahu, I remembered very well, hadn't said a word.) Now she would drag her by the hair. "Get up," she almost shouted, grabbing Suzana by the arm. Suzana's delicate arm looked as if it would break in that vice-like grip.

She pushed her roughly. Suzana's body seemed all out of joint. Her torso was thrust forward before her head could catch up, and her legs worked desperately to balance her again.

"So you've started already," the woman growled through clenched teeth. Then, just before leaving the cave, she turned to me.

"And you, you little wretch, you can't even blow your own nose yet . . ."

She called me other equally spiky-sounding names of the same general kind, with endings so sharp they sounded to me like they were laden with thorns.

They left. What would happen now? Would I have to go down into the wells?

Outside, it was calm and bright. A bird flew in the sky. The anger and the thorny words stayed behind in the gloom of the cave.

They're dragging me by the hair! What are you going to

do? . . . I walked slowly. My head felt numb. I couldn't get that wet rope near the edge of our cistern out of my mind. The black ashes in the bottom of the bucket still smelled of kerosene. "That's what comes from courting," Grandmother had said. "Oh Selfixhe, this was all we needed in times like these. Better death than love like this, may God protect us."

. . . dragging me by the hair, what are you . . . ?

I climbed up on the roof. From there I could see Suzana's house. The white sheets were hanging in the yard. The *juk . . .*

I lay down on the warm slates and looked up at the sky. A little cloud was drifting north. It kept changing its shape. "We can endure a lot, Selfixhe, but may God stop the spread of affairs of this kind. Better the plague."

Grandmother had gingerly picked up the bucket and emptied it. She stared for a long time at the wet black ashes, then shook her head. I was about to ask why she was shaking her head like that, but that handful of black ash robbed me of any inclination to speak.

The little cloud in the sky lurched ahead as if it was tipsy. It had turned long and skinny now. Life in the sky must be pretty boring in the summer. Not much happened then. The little cloud crossing the sky the way a man crosses an empty square in the noonday heat melted away before reaching the north. I had noticed that clouds died very fast. Then their remains drifted in the sky for a long time. It was easy to tell dead clouds from the living.

I was surprised to see Suzana the next day. She walked by our gate, accompanied by her father like a proper young lady. She didn't even turn to look at me. I thought she seemed completely alien. That evening, they passed by again. This time, when she saw me at the gate, she raised her head high and squeezed close against her father. Her father looked at me askance. He was very handsome.

In the days that followed, Suzana came out accompanied by her mother. Holding onto her arm like a proper young lady again. Her mother looked at me as you'd look at a mad dog. Who knows how many of those barbed-wire words were running through her mind, the old witch!

I spent the whole summer and the beginning of autumn at Grandfather's. It was the longest summer of my life. I was sleepy all the time. The days went by without incident and often without their names. When you'd unpacked the hours from the day and then the night and piled them all up, you could toss out the boxes they came in, which is all that "Wednesday" or "Sunday" or "Friday" really are.

The season dragged on. It started to get cold again. The first claps of thunder rumbled somewhere over the horizon. Babazoti's house got gloomier. Grandma quarrelled more and more with my younger aunt, who came and went happily, not paying the slightest attention to her mother, humming a song which had just come out:

> We're all so hungry and broke
> Townspeople and plain country folk . . .

Grandma would listen and shake her head thoughtfully, as if to say: "This girl will break my heart."

The first rain fell. It was time for me to go home. The sky was overcast. The wind blew in from the northern mountain passes. I went down Citadel Street, crossed the Bridge of

Brawls, and was making my way through the town centre. It felt funny to be among the grey stone walls rising high on either side. The streets were strangely empty. Except that in a little square near the market a small crowd of people stood listening to someone making a speech. I stopped to listen. I didn't know the speaker. He was a medium-sized man with greying hair who opened his arms wide from time to time as he spoke.

"In these times of turmoil we must try to love one another. Love will protect us. What can we gain from fratricidal struggle? Son will rise up against father, brother will fight brother. There will be rivers of blood. Let us drive civil war out of our town. Let us keep death out. For centuries the unhappy Albanian has gone through life with the heavy burden of a weapon on his back. Other nations think of food, but we Albanians care only for guns. Let us cast off that weight of steel, my brothers, for steel speaks only of strife. What we need is reconciliation. Civil war . . ."

The neighbourhood streets were completely deserted. The doors had a sly look about them. I walked faster. Where were all the people? I was almost running. My footsteps rang off the stones with a scary sound. More boarded doors. The metal door-knocker shaped like a human hand . . . No room at the inn! . . . But no, our gate, at least, stood ajar, waiting for me. I pushed it open and went in.

"You picked a great day to come back," my mother said.

"What do you mean?"

She didn't explain. Grandmother and Papa kissed me.

"Why did Mamma say I picked a great day to come back?" I asked Grandmother.

"They shot someone today," she said. "He was wounded."

"Who?"

"Gjergj Pula."

"Really? Who shot him?"

"No one knows. The police are looking for suspects."

"Did they ever find Aqif Kashahu's daughter?" I asked.

"What made you think of Aqif Kashahu's daughter?" Grandmother asked, almost reproachfully. "She's away visiting some cousins."

A partisan. A boy from the town centre had joined the resistance. A week before he had been a boy like all the others, with a home and a door with a knocker, who yawned when he was sleepy. He was Bido Sherifi's youngest nephew. And suddenly he had become a partisan. Now he was up in the mountains. On the march. The high peaks were shrouded in winter mists that rolled down the gorges like nightmares. The partisan was up there somewhere. Everyone else was down here. He alone was up there.

"Why do they say: 'He joined the resistance'?"

"You wear me out with your questions."

Start of winter. I was looking at the first frost that covered the world and wondering what foreign land's shreds and tatters would be blown to us by the winter wind this year.

XIV

Two truckloads of deportees were to leave that afternoon. The main square was swarming with people. Italian gendarmes came and went through the crowd. Heaped in the back of the trucks, the people who were being taken away had turned up the collars of their old coats. Many of them were holding little bundles, others were empty-handed. Almost all were silent. The crowd around them buzzed. Some women were crying. Others, especially the older ones, were giving advice. The men talked in low voices. The deportees kept quiet.

"What have they done? Why are they taking them away?" a passer-by asked.

"They spoke against."

"What?"

"They spoke against."

"What does that mean? Against what?"

"I'm telling you, they spoke against."

The passer-by turned away.

"Why are they taking them away? What have they done?" he asked someone else.

"They spoke against."

Bruno Arcivocale, commander of the city garrison, crossed the middle of the square, followed by a group of officers. There must have been a meeting at the town hall.

The truck engines had been idling for a long time. Then their monotonous hum in the square suddenly grew louder. The first truck revved up. Words spoken in loud voices, shrieks and cries came through the roar. The second truck also got into gear. The deportees waved. One of them shouted:

"Long live Albania!"

The square was full of excitement. In the end, the trucks made their way through a crowd that had surrounded them on all sides and drove off at speed.

The square emptied out. Apparently the meeting at the town hall had begun. Many guards were posted around the square. The streets were deserted.

Darkness fell on the city without those who had spoken against. Strangely enough, new leaflets were out that night. Lady Majnur left her house before dawn to report to the carabinieri.

Ilir came over that afternoon.

"Want to speak against?" he asked.

"Yeah, let's."

"But we have to be careful of spies," he added.

"Where should we go?" I asked.

"Up on the roof."

We went to Ilir's house and climbed up to the roof unobserved. The view was spectacular. Thousands of roofs stretched away endlessly, steep and grey, as though they had turned over and over in a fitful sleep. It was very cold.

"You start," Ilir said.

I took the lens from my pocket and put it over one eye.

"Dadadada, tatatata!" I said.

"Rabalama, paramara!" Ilir declared.

We sat and thought for a while.

"Long live Albania!" said Ilir.

"Down with Italy!"

"Long live the Albanian people!"

"Down with the Italian people!"

We fell silent. Ilir looked as though he had had a thought.

"No, that's not fair," he said. "Isa says the Italian people aren't bad guys."

"What's he talking about?"

"It's true. That's what he says."

"No," I insisted. "If their planes are bad, how can their people be good? Can a country's people be better than its planes?"

Ilir was shaken. He seemed ready to think again. But then just when he was about to change his mind, he said stubbornly, "No!"

"You're a traitor," I told him. "Down with traitors!"

"Down with the fratricidal struggle!" Ilir replied, putting up his fists as if he was about to box me.

We looked all around, automatically. We realised that we could easily have rolled off the roof.

Without another word we climbed down single-file and parted in anger.

Everyone was talking about the people who had joined the resistance. There were partisans from all the neighbourhoods, from Lower Palorto, Gjobek, Varosh, Cfakë, the central districts and the districts on the outskirts of town. But only one young girl had taken to the hills from Hazmurat.

Someone had brought news of the first casualty among the partisans. It was Avdo Babaramo's younger son. No one knew where he had been killed or how. The body had not been recovered.

Avdo Babaramo and his wife locked themselves in the house for several days. Then he hired a mule for three months, collected some money, and set out to look for his son in the mountains. He was up there now, moving around.

A war winter, that's what all the women who came to visit called it.

One day when I went to answer a knock at the door I was struck dumb. It was my maternal grandmother, who usually came to see us maybe once a year, since she was too heavy to make long journeys. And she never went out except in the spring, because she couldn't stand it if the weather was too hot or too cold. Yet here she was on our doorstep, her big face looking pale and worried.

"It's Grandma!" I called up the stairs.

My mother came running down the stairs, sick with worry. "What's happened?" she cried.

Grandma shook her head slowly. "Calm down," she said. "No one died."

Grandmother came to the top of the stairs and stood there like a statue.

"Welcome," she said calmly.

"Thank you, Selfixhe. It's good to find you all well."

Grandma was so out of breath from climbing up the stairs that she could barely get the sentence out.

We all waited.

The two grandmothers went into the main room and sat facing one another on the divans.

"My daughter," our visitor said through her sobs and tears, "my youngest has run off to be a partisan."

My mother sighed and sank onto the divan. Grandmother's grey eyes didn't blink.

"I thought it was something worse than that," my mother said softly.

Grandma continued to weep bitterly.

"A marriageable girl. Just when I was preparing her trousseau, she runs away, leaves everything. All alone in the mountains in this weather! She's only seventeen! Left all her embroidery half-done, strewn all over the house. Oh my God!"

"Get hold of yourself," said Grandmother. "I was wondering what on earth it could be. But look, she's with friends. She's gone, and crying won't bring her back. Let's just hope she comes back one day safe and sound."

Wet with tears, Grandma's face looked even more laughable.

"But what about the family's honour, Selfixhe?" she moaned. "What will people say?"

"Her honour will depend on the honour her comrades win," Grandmother said. "Make us some coffee, my child."

My mother put the coffee pot on the stove. I could hardly contain my joy. Taking advantage of the general turmoil, I slipped downstairs and ran over to Ilir's. I had completely forgotten that we were at loggerheads. He came out looking furious.

"Ilir, guess what! My aunt has joined the partisans."

Ilir was stunned.

"Really?"

I told him everything I knew. He looked thoughtful.

"Then why doesn't Isa go too?" he said at last, almost angrily.

I didn't know what to say.

"He's up in his room with Javer," Ilir said. "They sit around all day spinning the globe round and round."

We went upstairs. The door of Isa's room was ajar. Ilir went in first and I followed. They pretended not to notice us. Isa was sitting in a chair, chin on his fist, looking very annoyed.

"They know better than we do," Javer was saying.

"If they order us to stay here, it means that's what we have to do."

Isa said nothing.

"The front is everywhere," Javer said a moment later. "Maybe we're doing a better job by just staying where we are."

Silence again. The two of us stood stock still. The older boys were still pretending not to see us. Suddenly Ilir said, "How come you two don't go and join the partisans?"

Javer turned around. Isa seemed to freeze for a moment. Then suddenly he jumped up, spun around, and slapped his brother on the face.

Ilir put his hand to his cheek. His eyes glistened, but he didn't cry. We trooped out feeling mortified. We went downstairs in silence and walked out into the courtyard. The windows of Isa's room were right above our heads. We looked up in fury, then shouted:

"Down with traitors!"

"Down with civil war!"

Upstairs a door slammed. We ran off as fast as we could and found ourselves in the street.

By the time I got home, Grandma had gone.

In the days that followed, the only topic of conversation was about who had joined up. Every morning the women would open their shutters and exchange the latest news.

"Bido Sherifi's other nephew has taken to the hills as well."

"Really? Have you heard anything about Kokobobo's daughter?"

"They say she's gone off too."

"The word is that Isa Toska's people killed her."

"I don't know anything about it. Avdo Babaramo hasn't come back yet. He's still looking for his poor son's body."

"The poor old man. Wandering through the mountains in this winter weather."

Grandmother, Kako Pino and Bido Sherifi's wife were sitting on the sofas and sipping coffee when there was a knock at the door. To everyone's amazement, it was Lady Majnur.

"How are you, ladies? How are things? I thought I'd call. We haven't had a word since the air raids."

"Welcome, Majnur *Hanum*," my mother said.

Lady Majnur sat down next to Grandmother.

"I heard about your misfortune," said Lady Majnur, shaking her head. "A terrible blow, Selfixhe. Most unfortunate."

"Life brings many trials."

"True, Selfixhe, very true."

Lady Majnur's glassy eyes followed Mamma as she went to make the coffee.

"They've gone up to the mountains to join up, the bitches," she hissed.

No one answered.

My mother brought the coffee.

"Up in the mountains all the boys and girls sleep around without a second thought," said Lady Majnur. "Just wait. You'll see. They'll all come back with babies."

My mother turned pale. Lady Majnur's face grew harsher. A gold tooth in the right side of her mouth seemed to be smiling for all the others.

"But they'll catch them now, one by one," she went on. "They have nowhere to go. They've run out of food and clothing. In the middle of winter, with all the wolves. Anyway, they say a lot of them can hardly move. Obviously not. Pregnant to the eyeballs . . ."

"Come, Lady Majnur," said Grandmother. "Don't talk that way. Those stories might be slander."

There was a deep silence.

My mother turned away to hide her tears and went into the other room.

"You were harsh," said Grandmother.

Lady Majnur's glassy eyes tried to smile, but Bido Sherifi's wife stood up. Then she exploded:

"Dirty witch!" And she went to join my mother in the other room.

"The end of the world," said Kako Pino to no one in particular.

Lady Majnur stood up, puce with anger.

Grandmother did not budge. She was looking out at the winter-ravaged earth.

"Young boys and girls are getting together in the cellars to sing forbidden songs. They say they want to overthrow the old world and build a new one."

"A new world? What will this new world be like?"

"They're the ones who know, sister, they alone. But listen, come close and listen. They say that blood will have to be spilled for this new world to be built."

"That I can believe. If an animal has to be sacrificed when a new bridge is built, what will it take to build a whole new world?"

"A hecatomb."

"Good Lord! What are you saying?"

FRAGMENT OF A CHRONICLE

according to bulletin no. 1187. Countless Russian troops and tanks have been annihilated by the murderous fire of the Germans. A battle of apocalyptic scale. Only German and Italian troops, Mussolini has declared, could have endured a winter so harsh, the worst in a hundred and forty years. Timoshenko, wounded and bleeding, is roaming through the steppes of Russia, which are now piled high with corpses. Trial. Executive measures. Property. New evidence brought by the Karllashis. Gillette razor blades. Registered trademark. Safety blades. I hereby prohibit all assemblies in the streets, squares and houses. I order the suspension of weddings and funerals. Garrison commander Bruno Arcivo

XV

A notice was posted on what remained of a wall of the ruined house. We came to play in those ruins every day. Wallowing in their own misfortune, they were nonetheless kind to us. We took whatever we wanted from them, demolished small pieces of wall, shifted stones about, without much changing the look of the ruins. After enduring the flames, which had turned it into a ruin in a matter of hours, the house was now completely indifferent, and tolerated any fresh attack. Some iron bars protruding from the remnants of the walls looked like the fingers of a frozen hand. The notice had been hung right on those bars. Two old men had stopped to read it. It was typewritten, and in two languages, Albanian and Italian:

> Wanted: the dangerous Communist Enver Hoxha. Aged about 30. Tall. Wears sunglasses. Reward for any information leading to his capture: 15,000 leks; for his capture: 30,000 leks. Garrison commander Bruno Arcivocale.

Ilir tugged on the sleeve of my jacket.

"That was his house," he whispered to me.

"Enver Hoxha's?"

"Yes."

"How do you know?"

"I heard Papa telling Isa one day."

"So where is he now, this Enver Hoxha?"

"Far away. Somewhere near Tirana."

I whistled in amazement.

"He went all the way to Tirana?"

"Sure."

"Is Tirana very far?" I asked.

"Yes, very. Maybe we'll go there too when we grow up."

Someone else stopped to read the notice. We left.

Xhexho and Kako Pino were at our house drinking coffee with Grandmother. Xhexho carefully turned her cup upside down.

"It seems that a new kind of war has broken out," she said. "I forget exactly what they call it, war with classes or class war, or something like that. Well, Selfixhe, it's a war all right, but not like the others. In this war brothers kill each other. The son slays the father. At home, at the dinner table, wherever. The son looks his father in the eye, then he tells him he doesn't recognise him as his father any more and bang, he shoots him, right between the eyes."

"The end of the world," said Kako Pino.

"Apparently," Xhexho went on, "someone called Gole Balloma from the Gjobek neighbourhood is wandering the streets screaming that he's going to skin Mak Karllashi alive, cure and dry his hide in his own tannery, make shoes out of it and dance around in them."

"I've never heard anything so monstrous," my mother burst out in indignation.

"There you are, Selfixhe," said Xhexho. "We had thought

all our troubles were over, but now it looks as if the worst is yet to come. Do you remember Enver, the Hoxha boy?"

"The one who went to study in the land of the Franks? Of course I remember him?"

"And so do I," Kako Pino chimed in.

"Well, they say he's the one leading the war now. He's also the one who invented this new war I was telling you about."

"That's hard to believe," said Grandmother. "He was such a well-behaved lad."

"Yes, Selfixhe, very well behaved. But they say that he wears dark glasses now so he won't be recognised and that he's the one running the war."

"War, always war," Kako Pino sighed.

"What can you do?" said Grandmother. "It looks to me as if this world can't manage without war. As old as I am, I've never seen a day of real peace."

My mother sighed.

"I heard that Karllashi's daughter is back from Italy," Xhexho said, breaking the silence. "God, what a scandal! She wears her skirt above the knee and has dresses of such thin fabric you would think she was in a snakeskin. You can see everything. She spends all day preening, paints her lips red, bleaches her hair, smokes, and speaks Italian. 'Oh, Mother, what a filthy country,' she complains. 'Father, how could you bring me back to this hole.' Oh this, oh that, all day long. That's what the world's coming to, Selfixhe."

"What can you expect?" Grandmother asked once again. "That's what happens to girls when they leave home."

"Yes, exactly," Kako Pino agreed. "Everything's upside down."

The next day, as if he had been listening to Xhexho, Ilir said to me, "Let's go and have a look at Karllashi's daughter, the one who's just back from Italy."

"Is she pretty?"

"Very. Her hair is gold like the sun. She sits at the window daydreaming, and her hair blows in the wind."

We ran out, crossed Fools' Alley, and stopped in front of the Karllashis' house. And there she was, elbows resting on the windowsill, and it really did look as if she had sun in her hair. No other woman in the city ever had hair like that, except for one of the prostitutes, the one Ramiz Kurti had killed the year before, after which the brothel was closed for six months.

We stood in front of the Karllashis' house for a long time. Two *katenxhikas* went by. One was all hunched up. Then Gjergj Pula passed by. He was so pale he looked as though he had come straight out of hospital. We stared at each other. Then Maksut went by with a severed head under his arm. Karllashi's daughter left the window. We waited for her to reappear, but she didn't. Now we didn't know where to go. The street was deserted. Bido Sherifi's wife appeared at her window, shook flour from her hands, and disappeared. Nazo's door closed without a sound after Maksut went inside.

Suddenly shots rang out. A short burst. Then another burst. Then separate shots. Some people came running from Market Street, Harilla Lluka among them.

"Run!" he shouted. "Take cover! Someone's been killed."

Ilir's mother came to the doorstep.

"Ilir, get inside!" she yelled.

I heard them calling me, too. Doors were noisily slammed shut. More shots rang out.

The news spread like wildfire: Bruno Arcivocale, the garrison commander, had been assassinated.

Late that night the silence was broken by a knock at a door.

"It's at Mane Voco's," said Grandmother, going to open the window to look out.

Outside we heard heavy footsteps, then some words in Italian and shouts of "My son, my son!"

Then silence again. Someone had been arrested.

Grandmother closed the window.

"They just took Isa away," she said.

Arcivocale's funeral was magnificent. There were speeches in the centre of town. Then the long procession marched to the cemetery while a military band played. Shiny musical instruments wailed mournfully through their lily-shaped mouths. Fascist officers, dressed in black from head to toe, walked slowly alongside, looking impressive and serious. Followed by the priests. Then came the nuns. The casket containing Arcivocale swung gently from side to side. Old ladies, women and children rushed to a thousand windows. The city watched the departure of its late commander. On the walls, tatters of notices and ordinances torn by the wind would bear fragments of his name for some time: RCIV, ARC, OC, L. Then the rain would finally wipe them out and new notices and ordinances with the name of the new commander would go up.

It rained steadily for four days in a row. It was an ancient, monotonous rain. ("Once a rain fell upon the earth lasting thirty thousand years," Xivo Gavo said in the introduction to his chronicle.) It was under this rain that Isa was hanged. The execution took place at dawn in the town centre. Groups of people came to watch. Two girls were also hanged along with Isa. Their hair dripped with rain. Isa was missing one leg. It made him look horrible, like an upside down cone. His glasses were the only thing that seemed alive on his battered face. The victims had pieces of white cloth attached to their chests bearing their names. Azem Kurti, Javer's uncle and commander of the Balli Kombëtar, who along with Mak Karllashi's son had taken part in the killing of Isa, raised the skirts of the hanged girls with his cane. Their thin white legs swung back and forth for a moment before coming to rest. Mane Voco's wife broke away from the people trying to hold her back and ran through the streets screaming hysterically, "My son! My son!" She rushed all the way to the gallows and embraced Isa's single leg, pressing it to her face and hair. "My son, my son, what have they done to you?" The conical form gave a jerk. His glasses fell off. The woman gathered up the shattered lenses and pressed them to her breast. "My little boy, my little boy."

That same night, Javer, who was still a wanted man, went to his uncle Azem Kurti's house, where he had not set foot in a long time.

"They're looking for me, Uncle," he had said, "but I have repented."

"Repented? You have done the right thing, nephew. Come, let me kiss you. I knew this day would come. Did you see what we did to that friend of yours?"

"Yes, I saw," Javer answered.

"Bring us some raki and a hot meal," Azem said to the women. "Let us celebrate this reconciliation."

When they had sat down at the table, Javer said:

"Now, Uncle, you're going to tell me all about the business with Isa."

And Azem laid out the facts. Sipping his raki, eating his roast, he described the killing. Javer listened.

"What's wrong, nephew? You look pale," the uncle said.

"Yes, Uncle, I feel pale."

"Those books have thinned your blood. Your fingers are thinner too."

Javer looked at his fingers and then coolly took a revolver out of his pocket. Azem's eyes opened wide. Javer shoved the barrel of the gun into his uncle's food-stuffed mouth. Azem's teeth rattled on the metal. Then, one by one, the bullets smashed his jaw, his forehead and his skull to smithereens. Morsels of half-chewed meat mingled with blobs of Azem's brain as they rained down together onto the low dining table.

Javer left amid the wailing of his cousins. The next day, the Bulldog flew over the city dropping multi-coloured leaflets saying, "Yesterday the Communist Javer Kurti killed his own uncle at the family dinner table. Fathers and Mothers, judge for yourselves what the Communists are like."

That evening the bodies of six people shot dead in the citadel prison were brought to the main square. They were left there in a pile so people could see. A white banner bore this inscription in capital letters: THIS IS HOW WE ANSWER RED TERROR.

The rain had stopped. It was very cold at night. By dawn, the corpses were covered with frost. They lay there on the square all that day. On the second morning, another pile of corpses was found on the other side of the square. A bit of

cloth bore the words: THIS IS HOW WE ANSWER WHITE
TERROR.

The police rushed in to get rid of the bodies, but they
weren't given time to complete the job. They were ordered
to go after the terrorists first. None of the guards on duty the
previous night had suspected a thing. Around midnight, the
municipal road-sweeper's cart, drawn by Ballashi, an old nag
well-known to everyone in the city, had pulled up in the
square. As usual, the cart was covered with a black tarpaulin.
Just before daybreak someone passing alongside the cart
happened to give the tarpaulin an idle tug, and that's when
the bodies fell out in a heap.

People came back from the town centre in consternation.

"Go and see."

"Go and look, on the square. A real slaughter."

"Don't let the children see. Keep the children back."

Grandmother shook her head pensively and said: "What
terrible times."

The city was soaked in blood. The bodies of the executed
prisoners were still in the square. Now both piles had been
covered with tarpaulins. In the afternoon Hanko, a crone who
had not crossed the threshold of her house in twenty-nine
years, went out and headed for the centre of the city. People
were dumbfounded, and stepped aside to let her pass. Her
vacant eyes seemed to see everything without looking at
anything.

"Who is that man standing on that rock?" she asked,
pointing with her cane.

"It's a statue, Mother Hanko. It's made of iron."

"I thought it was Omer's son."

"It is Omer's son, Mother Hanko. He's been dead for a long time."

Then she asked to see the bodies. She went to each pile of corpses in turn, lifted the frozen tarpaulins, and stared at the dead for a long time.

"What country are they from?" she asked, pointing to the Italians.

"From Italy."

"Foreigners?" she said.

"Yes, foreigners."

She put her hands on each face, as if to recognise the corpses.

"What about those?"

"Those are from our city. This one is from the Toro family, this one from the Xhulas, this one the Angonis, this one the Merajs, and this one the Kokobobos."

Granny Hanko covered up the pile with her dry, withered hands and turned to leave.

"Why all this blood? Can't you tell us anything, Mother Hanko?" a woman asked between her sobs.

The crone turned her aged head, but seemed to have forgotten where the voice had come from.

"The world is changing blood," she said to no one in particular. "A person changes blood every four or five years, and the world every four or five hundred years. These are the winters of blood."

So saying, she set off homeward. She was one hundred and thirty-two years old.

Winter. White terror. Those words were everywhere. As was the frost. One day, I woke very early, got out of bed, and went upstairs to the main room. Thick clouds like wet, muddy sponges had settled over the city. The sky was black as pitch. A supernatural light spilled in through a single rent in the cloud cover. It slid over the grey roofs and came to rest on a white house. The only white building in the neighbourhood. I had never noticed that before. It looked sinister among the grey houses at that time of the morning.

What house was this? Where did it come from? And why do they call what's happening these days a "white terror"? Why not green terror, or blue terror?

I had grown more and more afraid of the colour white. The white roses I could remember, the drapes in the main room, Grandmother's nightgown — all now seemed inscribed with the word "terror."

FRAGMENT OF A CHRONICLE

rder. Any person found to have connections with the terrorists will be sentenced to death. I hereby declare a curfew from
four in the afternoon to six in the morning. Garrison
commander: Emilio de Fiori. Curfew exemptions previously
granted to midwives are hereby cancelled. I order a census of
the city pop

XVI

The highway, the bridge over the river, and Zalli Street teemed with soldiers, mules and trucks heading slowly north. Italy had capitulated. Long columns of soldiers with blankets on their shoulders were coming into the city. Some of them still bore their arms. Others had thrown them away or had sold them. The cobblestones were filthy with mud trampled in by their boots. The streets rang with shouting and swearing in Italian. The milling mass of soldiers got more and more chaotic. Some of them left straight away to go farther north, while fresh columns, each filthier than the last, arrived from the south. Rain-soaked, exhausted, and unshaven, the soldiers all trudged up steep Zalli Street, gazing in stupor at the tall stone houses.

The gloomy winter city looked down its nose at the defeated. Soon they too would wander through the snow like ghosts, mumbling *"pane, pane."*

Llukan the Jailbird with his blanket over his shoulder came down the road from the prison.

"Everyone's gone!" he was shouting. "Not a soul left in the prison. It's enough to make you cry."

The nuns left, too. The prostitutes had climbed aboard

a truck, and when it started off, Lame Kareco Spiri ran after it for a long time in the rain. Splattered by its rear wheels, he chased it madly, gesturing at the girls who, crammed into the back and whipped by the wind, waved back at him. When he finally gave up he walked back into the city looking utterly miserable and muttering unceasingly, "What am I going to do without them?"

Long, apparently endless columns continued to march along the highway. The whole city was spotted with mud.

"Disgusting, isn't it, Selfixhe?" said Aunt Xhemo, who had just arrived for a visit. "The world is one big mudhole."

"Well," said Grandmother, "that's the way kingdoms come to an end."

"Yes, they're leaving all right," said Aunt Xhemo, "but others will take their place, and leave their mud and filth behind."

The city had really been disguised by a mask of ugliness. The reddish-brown mud clashed with its distinguished tones of grey. The retreating Italians had muddied us all, just like the back wheels of the truck that carried off the ladies of the bordello.

I sat at the window in the main room two flights up and watched the routed army. The remnants of Greece had been scattered by the winter wind. Italy, on the other hand, was sunk in mire.

Grandmother and Aunt Xhemo, with their funny-looking ancient glasses with the cracked lenses perched on their noses, watched the road full of soldiers.

"Well, now Italy has been thrashed as well," Aunt Xhemo said. "They were a thorn in our side long enough."

"They didn't give us an easy time, that's for sure," commented Grandmother.

"Where will those poor lads go now, in the cold, and with so little to be had?" Aunt Xhemo asked.

"They'll be on the road," said Grandmother. "Where else can they go?"

"Pity the mothers waiting for them!"

"That's how it is when nations collapse in winter," said Grandmother.

Aunt Xhemo sighed.

"Blankets," she said a moment later, "a whole world of blankets."

The column of troops and mules kept on coming through the night. In the morning it stretched out just as far, making it seem as if yesterday's men and animals were still trudging past. Soiled with mud, the city awoke from a restless night to an even more troubled dawn. Isa Toska's gang had come into the city during the night, singing old songs. At dawn, they were followed by some Ballist detachments. In the morning the two groups, mixed in with the throng of harried Italian soldiers, wandered about almost side by side at the corners and squares, pretending not to notice one another. Here and there some scuffles broke out between Ballist patrols and Isa Toska's men.

Some Italian officers tried to fly off in the Bulldog, which had long been lying abandoned in the field. Sputtering and howling, the poor machine did manage to get a few metres off the ground in a lurching flight that ended with a crash in a field a few hundred metres away, and that last flight, as short as it was shameful, brought the history of the military airfield to a close.

But the real battle, the one Ilir and I reckoned ought to happen on the Bridge of Brawls, for we were sure it had been waiting for this for God knows how long so as to justify the name it bore, took place in fact around the Grihot barracks, pitting the Italians against the Ballists. The latter, taking advantage of the disorder and exhaustion of the Italians, tried to get them to disarm, initially by persuasion, then by force. Machine-guns went on spitting all day. That's when I first saw my father use Grandmother's opera glasses, to get a better view of what was going on over there.

My disappointment with the Bridge of Brawls persuaded me once and for all that, far from behaving in accordance with the meanings and responsibilities expressed by their titles or conventional names, people and things usually did the opposite. Ilir and I had begun to notice the phenomenon long before. Particularly since we had seen a group of gypsies with reed baskets on their heads raising not an eyebrow when they walked across the Ladies' Square, a place we thought reserved for the exclusive use of women of high rank.

I found it all very puzzling, but I stopped worrying about it when I heard Grandmother saying very firmly that the times we lived in were so full of distress that we would be hard put to say which was the worst of our troubles.

Right after the bloody clash at Grihot, the first detachment of partisans made its way across the airfield and came onto the road. The long thin column, with a red flag at its head, cut through the crowd of Italian soldiers, marched along Zalli Street, and went up into the city. A second column was coming down from the hills to the north.

A long cry came from afar: "The partisans! The partisans!"

I dashed up another flight to get a better look. The columns seemed very straggly to me. I had expected to see giants carrying gleaming weapons, but there were only those two ordinary columns — utterly ordinary columns — with the red flag at their head. Where were they going? Did they know that the city was angry and armed to the teeth? They could not have known, for they marched rapidly on to the centre of town. Then there was a third column, even sparser and less impressive, crossing the bridge through the crowds of Italian soldiers. That had a red flag, too.

Why weren't there more of them? Why didn't they have vehicles, artillery, anti-aircraft guns and a military band? Why only a red flag in front and a few mules carrying supplies and wounded bringing up the rear?

Now, as the first turned up Varosh Street, a fourth column was coming down a hill to the north. People rushed to the windows, shouting and waving kerchiefs. Someone played a harmonica.

I ran out into the street. They were coming closer now, pale and haggard, wearing outfits too big or too small. I scanned them, looking for my aunt. Look, there's a girl. Then another one with fair hair just like her. But no, it wasn't her. Then another. Not that one either. I didn't see Javer either. No one I knew. They were heading for the centre of town. Automatically, I fell into line beside them with a group of kids. Still no sign of my aunt. Maybe she was in another column. People shouted greetings from their windows. A group of women ran alongside the column, bombarding the partisans

with questions. Now and then one of the women would hug
a boy who had stepped out of the ranks.

The windows of Lady Majnur and the other agas' wives
were shut. I felt a vague anxiety. I was afraid that somewhere
further on lay a trap. And I had the feeling that the column
was walking right into it. The city was still crawling with
enemies. Isa Toska's gang of toughs, the Ballists with their
black moustaches, wide capes and white caps adorned with a
golden eagle, and the desperate horde of Italians, defeated but
still armed, all seemed to be waiting to cut that thin column
to pieces.

And up at the front, it did seem that something was
going on. I heard voices.

"Something's happened."

"At the minaret."

"What happened at the minaret?"

"His eyes."

"Whose eyes?"

"With a nail! A nail!"

"Send the children back inside!"

"Take the children away!"

We didn't want to go inside. For quite a while we had
been told more and more often to "get back inside, children."
The refrain was spoken so sternly that I wondered if our eyes
weren't what the city feared most of all. Ilir had gone so far
as to say that they would end up putting our eyes out! Unless
they covered them up with blindfolds and made us look like
pirates.

In the end, we had to turn back. Something really terrible
had happened. As the partisans approached the town centre,

Sheikh Ibrahim, who had climbed up the minaret to watch them arrive, had suddenly drawn a huge nail from his pocket and tried to put out his own eyes. Some passers-by had charged up the minaret and just managed to tear the bloody nail from his hands. Then they tried to make him come down, but, with his strength enhanced by his fury, he fought to take back the nail, screaming hoarsely at the top of his lungs, "Better no eyes at all than to see communism!" Finally, after repeated futile attempts to bring him down, the people trying to stop him, themselves in danger of falling off the tower, gave up and came down, leaving the sheikh alone up there. He stood with his chest pressing against the minaret's stone balustrade and, with his arms dangling over the edge, he began chanting an old hymn in a voice that made your blood run cold.

Night fell on a city full of Ballists, partisans, Isa Toska's men and a motley crowd of Italian troops. The night was thick with the sounds of orders, exclamations, passwords, horseshoes and footfalls. Halt! — Who goes there? — Death to the fascists! Freedom for the people! — Halt! *Non disturbare!* — We're Isa Toska's men. — Halt! Don't disturb me. — What's the password? — *Non disturbare, ché spariamo.* — Halt! — Freedom for the people! Death to traitors! Albania for the Albanians! — Get back! — Death to fascism! Don't shoot! — Halt! Get back I said! — Death to the *giaours!* — Halt!

The city was tossing and turning as if it were having a nightmare. It gave off a lugubrious rumble that was redolent with death.

At dawn, calm returned. It had stopped raining. The sky was grey, but very light grey. Bido Sherifi's wife was slipping down the alleyway.

"Aqif Kashahu has put on the Ballist uniform," she said, shaking the flour from her hands. "I saw him with my own eyes, the swine, all done up with leather cross-belts and ammo."

"A plague on him," Grandmother spat out.

Kako Pino pushed open the door.

"What's going on?" asked Aunt Xhemo, who had spent the night at our house. "I don't understand any of this."

"Who's in control of the city now?" Grandmother asked.

"No one," answered Kako Pino. "The end of the world."

The city was actually in the hands of the partisans. This became clear at about eight in the morning, when their patrols appeared everywhere. The Ballists had withdrawn to the Dunavat district. Isa Toska's gang had holed up in the Baba Selim mosque. The Italians held both sides of the main road, the river bed and part of the airfield.

It was quiet. Grandmother and Aunt Xhemo were sipping their morning coffee.

"They say the partisans are going to open communal or communist canteens of some kind," commented Aunt Xhemo dreamily.

Grandmother said nothing. She adjusted the glasses on her nose and looked outside.

"What's all that loud knocking?" she asked. "Go and look. I think it's coming from Nazo's."

She was right. There were three partisans. The one doing the knocking had only one hand, his left hand. The other two partisans were looking up at the windows. Nazo and her daughter-in-law appeared at one of them.

"Is this the residence of Maksut Gega?" asked one of the partisans.

"Yes, it is," said Nazo.

"Tell Maksut to come out right now," said the partisan.

"He's not home," said Nazo.

"Where is he?"

"Visiting some cousins."

"Open up. We'll look and see."

About fifteen minutes later they came out. The one-armed partisan took a small piece of paper from his jacket pocket, frowned, and started reading.

A minute later they were knocking on the main door of the Karllashi mansion. At first no one answered. They knocked again. Someone came to the window.

"Is this the residence of Mak Karllashi?"

"Yes, Mr Partisan."

"Tell Mak Karllashi and his son to come out!"

The head disappeared from the window. There was a pause. The other two partisans unslung their rifles. The one-armed partisan knocked again. It was an iron door and the knocks reverberated all around.

Finally there was a noise from inside. The sound of sobbing, and a woman's scream. The door opened halfway and Mak Karllashi came out first. Someone was trying to pull him back by the sleeve. "No, father, don't go out, don't go out!" He came out. He had black circles under his eyes. His daughter was hanging on his arm and refused to let go. The son, wax-pale, wearing polished black boots, came out after him. "Papa!" screamed the girl, clutching his arm. Behind the door a woman was crying.

"What do you want from us?" asked Mak Karllashi.

His long face shook to the rhythm of the jolts passed to his body by his daughter's sobs.

"Mak Karllashi, you and your sons have been sentenced as enemies of the people," the partisan said loudly, taking his gun from his shoulder with his one arm.

A howl came from behind the door.

"Who are you?" asked Mak Karllashi. "I don't even know you."

"The people's court," growled the partisan, and raised the barrel of his machine-gun.

The girl started screaming.

"I'm no enemy of the people," Mak Karllashi protested. "I'm a simple tanner. I make people's shoes, I make *opingas*."

The partisan looked down at his own tattered moccasins.

"Get out of the way, girl," he shouted, aiming his gun at the man. The girl screamed.

"Put down that gun, you dog," she said blankly.

"Out of the way, bitch," the partisan said, levelling the gun at the two men.

"Wait a minute, Tare," said one of the partisans as he moved to draw the girl aside. But he didn't have time.

"Death to communism!" shouted Mak Karllashi.

The gun of the one-armed partisan fired. Mak Karllashi went down first. The partisan tried to miss the girl, but in vain. She writhed tight against her father as if the bullets had stitched her body to his. After the burst of fire came a muffled silence. The bodies had fallen in a heap. They twitched for a moment, then seemed to find peace. The shiny black boots of the tanner's son protruded from the pile of silent bodies.

The sound of wailing came from behind the door.

"Roll me a cigarette," the one-armed partisan said to his friend. He looked upset.

After a while they slung their weapons on their shoulders again. They were about to leave when heavy footsteps sounded on the cobblestones. It was a partisan patrol. Three of them, all tall, and wearing studded boots. They approached.

"Death to fascism!"

"Freedom for the people!"

"What happened here?" asked the one in the middle.

"We just executed an enemy of the people," the one-armed partisan said.

"The order?" said the partisan sternly.

Partisan Tare took the crumpled piece of paper from his pocket.

"Fine," the other said.

The three men turned to leave, when at the last moment one of them noticed Mak Karllashi's daughter's hair in the pile.

"Let me see that order again," he said, turning to Tare.

Partisan Tare looked him in the eye. He reached slowly, very slowly, into his jacket pocket with his one arm and felt with two fingers for the piece of paper.

The partisan from the patrol read it dutifully.

"I see a girl was executed here," he said. "I don't see her name on the order."

"It's not there," said Partisan Tare, and his neck stiffened as though he'd been slapped.

"Who shot her?"

"I did."

"Your name?"

"Tare Bonjaku."

"Partisan Tare Bonjaku, put down your weapon," the patrol leader ordered. "I'm putting you under arrest."

Partisan Tare lowered his head.

"Your gun."

His hand moved again. He shrugged the strap off his shoulder and held out the gun.

The other man began looking around. His gaze stopped at the courtyard of Xuano's abandoned house.

"Over there," he said, pointing to the courtyard.

Partisan Tare started for the courtyard.

"You, keep him here under arrest until the comrades come to give judgment," he said to Tare's two companions.

"Yes, sir."

"Death to Fascism!"

"Freedom for the people."

The arrested partisan sat down on a pile of stones and looked at the walls of the abandoned house, which had begun to collapse.

His companions sat some distance away. No one spoke. Outside, the cries of the Karllashi women could still be heard. They were dragging the bodies into their own yard. The arrested man asked for another cigarette. They gave it to him.

He smoked it, then sat with his chin in his hand. The two others looked away. Finally footsteps were heard in the street. They had arrived. There were three of them.

The man under arrest stood up. It was a short trial.

"Partisan Tare Bonjaku, you are accused of killing a girl. Is it true?"

"It's true," he answered.

"What do you have to say in your defence?"

"Nothing. I have only one hand. The enemies of the

people cut off my right hand. I don't shoot well with the left. I hit the girl by accident."

"We understand."

They conferred privately for a moment. Then one of them spoke:

"Partisan Tare Bonjaku, you are sentenced to death by firing squad for the misuse of revolutionary violence."

Silence. The man who had just spoken gestured to Tare's two companions.

"Now?" one of them asked in a faint voice.

"Yes, now."

Their foreheads were wet with cold sweat.

The condemned man understood. He remained near the walls and looked at them. They took their weapons from their shoulders. He raised his one arm in a clenched-fist salute and shouted:

"Long live communism!"

A brief burst of fire. The partisan fell onto the pile of stones.

They left, with the dead man's two companions bringing up the rear.

"We lost Tare for a filthy whore," one of them muttered.

"They're killing each other now!" someone shouted in the distance. "They're killing each other now!"

Lady Majnur stuck her head out of the window and made a face.

"As long as they carry on to the last man!"

The two partisans heard her and looked up immediately, but there was no one in the window. One of them raised his machine-gun and fired a burst at the windows. Shattered panes spattered noisily on the cobblestones.

OLD SOSE'S NEWS
(in lieu of a chronicle)

It is written in the ancient books: "A people with yellow hair will try to reduce this city to ashes."

XVII

The German troops had crossed the southern border and were now marching towards the city, from which the citizens were fleeing. It was the third time in its long history that the city had been abandoned in this way. A thousand years before, the inhabitants had fled when plague struck. The second time was four centuries ago, when the imperial Ottoman army crossed the border under the banner of Islam, at the same place where the German troops were now on the march.

The city was evacuated. You could feel the great loneliness of the stone.

Monday night was full of voices, footsteps, the slamming of doors. Groups of friends and neighbours were getting ready, locking the heavy doors and setting out in the middle of the night for outlying villages.

Mane Voco and Bido Sherifi, with their wives and children, had gathered in our hallway, along with Nazo and her daughter-in-law. Maksut had disappeared. I was sad because of Grandmother. She wouldn't come with us this time either. Nor would Kako Pino. She was afraid there would be a wedding while she was gone. Someone might call her. For sixty years she had made up the city's brides. She couldn't let them down now. A badly made-up bride was the ugliest thing on earth, the end of the world, she had protested when they tried to persuade her to leave. No, no, no.

We left. We walked with faltering steps, like drunk-ards. Here and there in the darkness we could hear other steps. The town was draining itself of people. At the outskirts of the city we found ourselves alone. Bido Sherifi led the way, cane in hand. My father kept stumbling on the stony road. The others muttered, cursed, swore, coughed, and twisted their ankles in the ruts. Only Nazo's daughter-in-law walked gracefully, even in that sinister night, swaying very slightly. I guess she couldn't walk any other way.

We passed the fields lying fallow. When the moon came out, we were on the high road. I had never seen anything so dismal as the road that night, with its endless ruts dug by the truck wheels. In the moonlight, they looked like the black rails of a line leading towards death. Nazo stumbled, fell, and got up again.

We crossed the bridge over the river. The deserted airfield lay before us.

We had to cross over it. We came to its edge. I never thought I would walk on it one day. It saddened me greatly. In our eyes that field had something sacred about it. It had been a kind of sister or bride to the sky. Chosen by fate, like a princess. Now it was sundered from the sky like a wife scorned, and it had a wild and gloomy mien.

From all around came the smell of manure. Resentful cattle had soiled the airfield. I was now convinced that weeds and cattle and mud would always win out in the end — never the sky.

Farther along, we could make out Holy Trinity hill, and just behind it, black and menacing, strangely close as though it had risen up suddenly to see who was coming, loomed the dark bulk of the mountain.

Auntiemoon Pino tried hard to improve the view or at least to embellish and soften the sinister look of the landscape. But its light, greedily sucked up by the mud and fog, was so faint and weak that it only sullied everything even more.

Finally the moon disappeared behind the clouds.

"We can't see a thing," said Nazo's daughter-in-law.

Everyone turned round to look. She was right, the city was blotted out completely.

Someone moaned.

Now the plain, the road, Holy Trinity hill, the nameless banks of fog, and the mountain itself (it was hard to believe we were walking towards a mountain, for its shape was so ill-defined that it seemed that all we had before us was a slightly thicker patch of night) began shifting about awkwardly, scratching themselves in the dark like prehistoric monsters. Little by little I lost all sense of reality. We were walking aimlessly, walking for the sake of walking, wandering in the belly of the night. I could no longer think. I was used to thinking between walls, at street-corners, in rooms, and these familiar places seemed to give order to my thoughts. But now, without them, everything was not only incomprehensible, but cruel, too. The mountain leaned right over Holy Trinity hill and calmly chewed its neck. The hill gave up the ghost. Someone sneezed. The sound cheered me but not for long.

The moon came out again. The mists were drawn immediately to its light, drank it into their beards and let it drip back onto the muddy mess of the field. Caught in the act, the mountain hastily drew back from the hill, but a deep gouge in the hill's neck was clearly visible.

Nazo's daughter-in-law, the only one who had not sighed or moaned even once during the walk (maybe because she was walking through the kingdom of magic, with whose ways she had long been familiar), looked back again.

"The city," she muttered.

"Where?" I asked softly.

"There."

"That mist?"

"Yes."

That's where Grandmother was.

The moon disappeared again, taking my thoughts of Grandmother with it. Taking advantage of the darkness, the mountain bent over the hill again. This time it would surely strangle it to death.

We walked on like that for a long time. Now we were going up a steep slope.

"Don't fall asleep," said Bido Sherifi.

Ilir was alongside me.

"I was sleeping," he admitted.

"How?"

"I don't know."

We were still going uphill.

"It's getting light," said Mane Voco.

It was true, there was a faint light in the sky, but it looked as though it might change its mind and darken again at any moment.

We stopped to rest on a small plateau. The plain below, the road, the hills, the mists and the mountain were now slowly beating back the power of night. Exhausted, still pale with anguish, they awaited the morning.

"Look," Ilir said, "Look over there."

In the distance, the contours of the city could just be seen in the murky mix of night and day. It was the first time I had seen it from afar. I almost shouted for joy, for all night I had had the feeling that it was sinking lower and lower into the mud of the plain, like an old ship foundering on the shore.

But now the contours of the landscape had finally flung the impish genies from their back and were gradually recovering their shapes in the daylight. Only the grey eyes of Nazo's daughter-in-law still held something of the magic of the night.

The city was far away, caught in the clumsily opening jaws of the fog. The crones were down there. Grandmother and Aunt Xhemo, with their cracked glasses perched on their noses, were keeping watch over the road from their respective windows, waiting to catch a glimpse of the men with yellow hair. Clues had been perceptible for some time. Now the signs were unmistakable: Grandmother and Aunt Xhemo were getting ready to turn into crones. The German invasion seemed to be the definitive test for them, as the great incursions of the Turks, the massacres on the ruins of the republic and the monarchy, and the forty years of constant hunger had been for other crones.

"Let's move," said Bido Sherifi. "We're nearly there."

We got up. I was almost asleep on my feet. It was a painful slumber, cut and torn by the jolts passed to my body by the holes in the road.

Then someone said, "This is it. We're here."

I opened my eyes.

"We're here!"

"Where?"

"Here."

I had no idea where I was.

"In the village?"

"Yes, in the village."

"Where is it?"

"Right there."

I looked around in bewilderment. So this was what they called a village! I was dumbfounded, then suddenly burst out laughing.

"What's the matter? What's wrong with you?" asked Nazo's daughter-in-law.

I couldn't stop laughing.

"Lord above, now my child's lost his mind!" my mother said.

"What's the matter with you?" my father asked sternly.

"But . . . don't you see? . . . those houses . . . over there?"

"Now stop that," my father commanded.

My mother shook me by the shoulders, then put her arms around me.

I couldn't believe what I was seeing. These low shacks with whitewashed walls looked to me like dolls' houses. They weren't even lined up in a row so as to form one side of a street facing the other side in a virtually permanent state of rivalry, taunting each other with a sneering challenge: "So you want to see who's bigger, do you?" No, it was all different here. To prevent such squabbling, the cottages were separated from each other as if they were all in business on their own accounts. And to top it all, they were surrounded by patches of tilled land, chicken coops, haystacks and doghouses.

The villagers stared in amazement as our little group made its way across an open space. Two or three frightened kids hid behind their doors. A cow began to moo. More peasants came out. They had kindly features, the sun was in their hair, and they smelled of fresh milk.

I could hear cowbells tinkling. My eyes closed.

I woke up halfway through the afternoon. I was in an empty room. My father was hanging paper over the windows to replace the broken panes, while my mother cleaned the floor, which was filthy with dried-out chicken droppings. It all seemed very depressing to me.

In a little while Bido Sherifi's wife and Nazo came.

"So, are you settled in?" they asked.

My mother pursed her lips.

"What about you?"

"Not so bad. We found an abandoned house."

Bido Sherifi's wife heaved a deep sigh.

"How did we get into this mess?"

They left.

I felt like crying. Suddenly I was terribly homesick for our house and the city. Had something irreparable happened?

Papa went down to the cellar and came back up.

"Be careful not to light a fire," he said. "It's full of hay down there. If it goes up we'll burn like mice in a barn."

Mane Voco came by. He had lost a lot of weight since Isa was hanged.

"Do you have a little salt?" he asked. "We forgot to bring any."

My mother gave him some.

The house we were in was also abandoned. The other room was a wreck. I went downstairs to see the hay.

"A-oo," I said at the cellar entrance.

There was no answer.

The hay we were worried about had a heady tang. I went back up to the room wondering why we always lived in houses with some danger underneath. In the city it was the water in the cistern, here the threat of fire in the cellar.

Refugees from the city passed by all day. Some stopped in the village and moved into deserted houses like we had. Most kept going, looking for villages farther away. I noticed Qani Kekezi among the people walking by with bundles and cradles. Bits of newspaper, cigarette butts and gossip trailed in the refugees' wake. Back in the city Gjergj Pula had been killed. He had just applied to change his name again, to Jürgen Pulen. (The rumour was that apart from Giorgio, Yiorgos and Jürgen, which he never got a chance to use, he had lined up the name Yogura in case of a Japanese invasion.)

Refugees passed through the villages all night long. I slept fitfully, a sleep interrupted by tinkling bells, the lowing of cattle, and knocking at doors.

I was still asleep when I heard Xhexho's loud voice from the street.

"Where are you, my friends? I've been looking for you everywhere. Where are you, poor things?"

She burst in the door. Bido Sherifi's wife and Ilir's mother ran to her.

"Xhexho, do you have any news? What's happening?"

Xhexho started pacing up and down the room, then brought her hands to her cheeks.

"My God, how low we have fallen! Wandering the road like Romanies. Scattered like a raven's chicks. What kind of a pigsty is this? How did you end up here? Why has God let us live, to be reduced to this? What a catastrophe!"

"Enough, Xhexho! It's not as if we took to the road for the fun of it. We had no choice but to flee evil," said Bido Sherifi's wife. "What news have you brought?"

"I don't know where to start. Did you hear what happened to Çeço Kaili's daughter? She went off with the Italians."

"With the Italians?"

"Lately, her beard got as long as Mullah Kasemi's. The barber was at Kaili's house every day with a bag full of all kinds of razors, even the ones the Franks make. There was no other choice. Nothing else worked. Then one night she just got up and left. They say it was the barber who set it up. She got into the truck that took the girls from the brothel."

"Maybe the terrible bad luck that has befallen the city has left with her," said Xhexho. "After all, that girl with the beard did bring bad luck. It's a good thing she left," Xhexho added, surprising everyone with the uncharacteristically hopeful words she had spoken. But her optimism was short-lived. Raising her voice, which sounded like a dull whistle coming through her nose, she nearly shouted, "No, it won't leave us alone just yet! Have you heard what they're saying about Maksut, Nazo's boy? He's a spy! Yes, a spy!"

"A spy?"

"That's what I said. A snake in the wall. That's why he let his wife and mother come here alone; he's afraid of the partisans. He's in hiding, hasn't turned up anywhere. They say he's waiting for the Germans. He sends them information at night and tells them which roads to take. They say he's the one who reported Isa."

Ilir's mother broke into sobs.

"The cur, the cur," she cried.

Xhexho sighed deeply.

"Avdo Babaramo still hasn't found his son's body," she said in a less excited voice. "The poor man is still on the road, looking everywhere. But now we're all on the road." Xhexho raised her voice and added: "Like wandering Jews!"

Her nasal voice droned on. Then, obviously worn out, she spoke more softly.

"What can I say? We left home like crazy people. Men and women loaded down with bundles, cradles, bowls, and the infirm, and our dogs and cats ran off without a second thought, like the wretched of the earth. And Dino Çiço among them, with his plane on his back."

"With his plane?"

"Yes, dear friends, with his plane on his back! His family followed along behind, begging him to leave it in the house, saying he wouldn't be able to take the weight and would slow them all down. But he wouldn't hear of leaving it behind. He wouldn't risk the Germans getting hold of it for anything in the world."

Grandmother's absence became painfully clear. Only she could do anything to keep Xhexho from going on and on. Nothing my mother or any of the other women could say had any effect on Xhexho's unstoppable rant.

Xhexho sensed this and savoured her position.

"So there you are, my dears. We have all been swept up by a miserable fate. You'll never be able to call me a Cassandra again! When men got into planes, Xhexho said nothing. She was downcast, but kept her trap shut. But now we have a plane that has got onto a man! No, no and no! That is a monstrosity which drives me to distraction!"

Egged on by her own eloquence, she raised her voice and her rhetoric to its highest pitch.

"Oh Lord, what have we done to make You harry us so? You dropped bombs on us. You made our beards grow. You caused black water to rise from the earth . . . What tribulations will you visit on us next?"

At the climax of her declamation, Xhexho vanished into thin air, as she always did.

For the first time in my life I thought she was right. I had long suspected that everything was about to go upside down. Had our own cellar not challenged the main room of the house? Had not the beard destined for Jur Qosja's chin gone and planted itself on the face of Çeço Kaili's daughter? Not to mention those resentful cows that had got their own back on the aeroplanes . . .

I could not stop thinking about Dino Çiço tramping through the night with his plane on his back. But the two of them had probably fallen out. Their relationship must have soured, like everything else these days.

I ran outside hoping to see him and his plane. It was cold. There weren't many refugees. The few I saw could hardly move. I recognised two boys from the neighbourhood.

"Where are you staying?" I asked.

"Over there, in that little shack. What about you?"

"In this one here."

We didn't use the word "house."

Finally I found Ilir. He had looked haggard ever since Isa's death. I told him what Xhexho had said about Maksut. His eyes flashed with hatred.

"Listen," he said to me. "When we go back to the city, we'll kill Maksut, OK?"

"OK. There's an old dagger at home that belonged to my grandfather."

"Is it sharp enough?"

"Yes, it's really sharp. It even has Turkish writing on the handle."

"We'll ambush him at night on his way home. I'll jump on his neck and you get him with the knife."

I thought for a while.

"It's better if we invite him to dinner and kill him in his sleep, like Macbeth did," I said. "Then we'll salt his head."

"And roll it down the stairs so the right eye pops out," Ilir added. "But wait a minute. How can we invite him to dinner? Where?"

We started making very intricate plans. We were almost happy. Qani Kekezi passed alongside us. His plump and ruddy face looked smooth, but closer examination revealed some fresh scratches.

"The poor village cats are in for it now," Ilir said.

I laughed. I was happy to have my friend back. It seemed to me that Isa's death had made him grow up and leave me behind. But now we were together again.

While plotting our assassination, we had walked to the outskirts of the village without realising it. The ground was covered with frost. All around us, trees whose names we didn't know, birds we were seeing for the first time, irregular, scattered haystacks, the crumbling earth softened by the ploughshare, cowpats — everything was as strange to us as it was incomprehensible. Some village children with soft eyes looked at us timidly. I looked at Ilir's thin, drawn face and his untidy bush of hair and it occurred to me that I must look more or less the same. The peasant kids started following us.

"Did you see how frightened of us they were?" asked Ilir. "We're frightening."

"We're killers!" I said.

I took out the lens and put it over my eye.

"*Thou canst not say I did it: never shake thy gory locks at me!*" I thundered, addressing a half-eaten haystack.

"What's all that?" Ilir asked.

"That's what we'll say when Maksut's ghost appears after the murder."

"That'll be *formidable*," Ilir said.

The village children who followed us were shivering. Now we were walking on a ploughed field.

"Why is the earth soft? What did they do to it?" Ilir asked, trying to sound angry.

I shrugged.

"Peasant work," I said.

"Work with no rhyme or reason."

"None whatsoever."

"Let's plan the murder instead," said Ilir.

The peaceful plateau, which lay on a gentle incline, was exposed to the winter winds. The haystacks scattered here and there added to the impression of calm. We walked among them, talking about the details of our murder. Without thinking, we soon found ourselves on the main road. Peasants and mules mingled with the refugees. Other people were coming from the opposite direction. A sallow-looking woman struggled to stay astride a mule.

"Not far from here there's a monastery where they cure the sick," Ilir said.

We turned back towards the village. We were following a group of refugees who, according to what we heard them saying, were coming back from the monastery, which they had gone to visit just out of curiosity. Others were coming towards us, on their way there.

"Where are you going?" someone in the crowd walking along with us asked them.

"To the monastery," they answered, "to see the hand that works miracles."

"Some miracles! We're just on our way back from there. You know what it is? It's the English pilot's arm."

"The Englishman's arm?"

"The very same. With that ring still on the finger. Remember? It was stolen from the museum."

"Of course. So that's what happened to it."

"You may as well go back."

They turned back. We walked along absentmindedly among the chattering crowd. Then, little by little, there were fewer and fewer words, until the only sound came from our own footsteps.

"That arm," someone said in a dull voice. "It's as if it's following us."

No one answered.

"Poor humans," the same voice said again. "If they only knew where their heads and hands can end up."

We were back in the village.

At dusk, far in the distance where the city must have been, flames shot up. The refugees all came out and silently watched the pale flickering. We thought they were burning houses belonging to partisans. Through the gathering dark-ness and mist, the city waved its flame handkerchiefs, sending signals whose meaning no one could guess.

We kids climbed a barren knoll and shouted at the top of our lungs.

"That one up there is my house! That's my house burning! Hurrah!"

"It's not true. It's mine, it's my house."

"Who in your family joined the resistance?"

"My uncle."

"My brother's a partisan too!"

Then we started arguing about the size of the flames. Each of us boasted that the flames from his house were higher than all the others.

"Mine's the one all that smoke is coming from. One time when the chimney caught fire . . ."

"Smoke doesn't count."

"If you want to see something, just wait till my house burns."

"Yeah, wait till my Grandfather's Turkish books go up; they're as thick as baklava," I said proudly.

"Wait till my grandmother catches fire! She's got so much fat on her she'll go up like a torch," said Lady Majnur's grandson.

"Shame on you! How can you talk about your own grandmother that way?"

"She's a Ballist, my grandmother is."

"Ilir!" his mother called, "Ilir!"

One by one, we all peeled away. As I was about to go back I saw Nazo's daughter-in-law sitting all alone on a bare hillock, wearing a lovely jacket with a fur collar. The moon had just come out, and her pretty head stood out from the white fur collar as though from mist.

"Good evening," she said to me.

"Good evening."

She put her hand on the nape of my neck and ran her fingers through my hair, which had not been cut for a long time.

Then suddenly she asked me:

"What have you heard about Maksut?"

I looked down and didn't say anything. Her fingers stiffened for a moment on my neck, then relaxed their grip.

"It's burning," she said, looking off towards the fires. "Are you sorry?"

I didn't know what to say.

"Well," she said, "I hope it all burns down *entirely*." (The word "entirely" sounded strange on her lips.) "So that nothing's left but ruins. Do you like ashes?"

I was dumbfounded.

"Yes," I said.

At that moment, in the moonlight, her eyes looked to me like two magical ruins.

Who are you then? How come you don't know the birds, haystacks or trees? Where do you come from?

We come from that city over there. What we know about is stone. They're like people, stones are: they're young or old, hard or soft, polished or rough, sharp, pink and pock-marked, pitted or veined, sly or dependable enough to hold your foot when you slip, faithless, glad at your misfortunes, faithful, remaining on duty in foundations for centuries, dull-witted, morose, proud, dreaming of bearing epitaphs, modest, devoted without hope of reward, lined up on the ground in endless cobblestone rows like nameless people, nameless to the end of time.

Are you serious or crazy, or what?

And now, just like people, they're splattered with blood by the war.

Lord, what kind of a city is that?

A city of the ordinary kind.

Ordinary? No, that's not a city at all. It is an abomination.

WORDS OF UNKNOWN PERSONS

Don't give me that about yellow hair. Who knows what's under those iron helmets? They march. They march. Fighting rages everywhere. Where are we going in the darkness like this? I can't stand it any more. Some day it will be beautiful, the sky will be clear. Where are you going? It is snowing in the mountains.

XVIII

At break of day, in the far distance, the city awoke, all alone and moody. Though it seemed very far away, on its fate depended everything around it: the mountains, the villages and the valleys. Fire in the city was an alarm signal for the whole surrounding area. Now, half deserted, like a prehistoric city in which life had ceased long ago, the nearly empty stone shell awaited the Germans.

The road that would lead them there (as it had led so many armies) now writhed at the city's feet, begging forgiveness. But the city, proud and haughty as always, did not so much as glance at it. Through its clouded windows, it gazed out at the horizon.

At first, no one knew what had happened when the German reconnaissance patrol reached the city gates. We only found out later. The patrol was met with rifle-fire and grenades. The surviving motorcyclists turned back as quick as a flash. Then the road remained deserted for a while, sunk in a deep silence. The city had observed the time-honoured custom, and now calmly awaited reprisals.

They were not long in coming. This time tanks led the way. The road was black with them. The tanks did not enter the city but stopped on the road, and only their long gun-barrels turned slowly towards the city. The Germans waited for some time, expecting to see white flags go up. But all remained grey.

Then the shelling began. It made a heavy, monotonous, pounding noise. The whole valley was filled with the sound of iron smashing against stone. Broken pieces of walls and roofs, the limbs of houses and the heads of chimneys, flew in all directions. Grey-black dust settled over everything. Two men who tried to raise a white flag atop one of the houses were shot dead by others determined not to surrender. A third man, snaking his way across a roof dragging a white bed-sheet, was hit as he tried to unfurl it. He collapsed on it, and as he rolled down the gradient he wound himself in the sheet as in a shroud, then plummeted to the street below.

The shelling lasted for three hours. Finally, in the midst of the grey backdrop of death, someone managed to wave something white. No one ever found out who it was that rose up like a ghost over the city only to sink back down into the abyss after waving that white something at the Germans. Exactly what it was no one knew — a flag, a handkerchief, or maybe just a headscarf. What was certain was that this white thing would long stick in people's minds.

The Germans, apparently observing the target through binoculars, immediately caught sight of the white patch which clashed with the chaos of dust and debris. The shelling stopped. The tanks swung their gun turrets and began climbing up towards the city. The whole earth trembled. The tank treads clanked, echoed and struck sparks as they flayed the cobblestones. The air was filled with a hellish din. The nearly abandoned city had been invaded.

It was later learned that just when the tanks were rolling up Great Bridge Street into the city, roaring like monsters, Aunt Xhemo and the crone Granny Shano were standing at their windows talking to each other.

"What's all the noise for?" Aunt Xhemo had asked. "They could just as well have come in without all that ruckus."

Granny Shano had replied:

"They all make a lot of noise on the way in. But when they leave, you don't hear a thing."

At dusk, the city, which through the centuries had appeared on maps as a possession of the Romans, the Normans, the Byzantines, the Turks, the Greeks and the Italians, now watched darkness fall as a part of the German empire. Utterly exhausted, dazed by the battle, it showed no sign of life.

Night fell. After the thunder that had swept over the whole region in waves, the world seemed deaf. In the restored calm, the thousands of refugees scattered through the surrounding villages and countryside, who had watched and listened to what was happening, stood as if turned to stone.

What was the city doing now, up there in the dark, alone with the Germans? According to the prophecies, this was to be the last year of its millenary life. The men with yellow hair had finally come.

In the village where we were staying hardly anyone slept that night. We all stood outside, silent and expectant. The very few who went inside to nap soon came out again, wrapped in their blankets. No one spoke or raised his voice. All eyes were turned to where they thought the city was. It was deep in black. Iron tank claws were sunk into its chest. No light. No signal. It was being strangled in darkness.

But daybreak came, and it was still there. Grey, as always, and big. Someone was crying. One word was on everyone's lips: "tonight." We had decided to go back.

That evening we left the village. The same people were in our group. But Xhexho had joined us too. We walked in silence, leaving behind the haystacks that cropped up here and there. They seemed to want to tell us something, but couldn't. We were strangers.

At the same time refugees were returning to the city in small groups from every direction. In a few hours, the gigantic half-deserted shell would again be filled with footsteps, murmurs, passionate speeches, gossip, hopes and suffering.

We walked without stopping. We had long since passed the last haystack.

"Let's turn back," Xhexho said suddenly, stopping dead. "There's a ringing in my right ear."

No one said anything. We walked on. Xhexho went on mumbling for a while.

"Where are you rushing, you unhappy people?" she said tearfully. "To your doom!" An old woman from among the Hankonis told her to shut up. And so she did.

We marched on. It was maybe midnight. We could see nothing. We sensed that boils and tumours had sprouted here and there in the night. Probably knolls and boulders.

It must have been after midnight when we came down to the plain. A black shape loomed near us: the wreck of the Bulldog. There was an acrid smell. Someone must have used it as a latrine.

"Do you remember where you hid the dagger?" asked Ilir.

"Yes," I told him.

We stopped to rest. Ilir and I went to piss near the downed plane. I never would have believed we could do such a thing.

Day was dawning, and little by little the contours of the city were vaguely taking shape. It loomed before us like a sphinx. We weren't sure what to do. Should we go in or not? Chimneys, rooftops and windows were emerging one after another from the blackened chaos. The spires of minarets and bell-towers and the tin flashings of gable-ends looked like madmen wandering among the roofs in ancient helmets.

We decided to go in. We crossed the river bridge (the sentry post had been abandoned) and took the road. There were no Germans anywhere. Maybe they were holed up in the citadel.

We still had a way to go across uncultivated fields. Suddenly the city rose up right in front of us. High and steep, almost vertical. Looking disdainful. Maybe a bit offended at having been deserted. Signs of the battering it had taken were everywhere: shattered house-fronts, demolished balconies.

We noticed a white patch on the first telegraph pole. As we came closer we saw that it was an announcement. It was still dark and we could barely make out the words. "I order . . . the arrest of . . . pers . . . dead . . . three . . . shot . . . as well as . . . garrison commander: Kurt Vollersee."

We were on our way up Varosh Street. A faint light glimmered in the window of Xivo Gavo, the chronicler. Suddenly I felt a hand pull my head and press it against someone's bosom.

"Don't look!"

A dark shape was visible on one side of the street. Like

a contorted body. I couldn't really tell what it was. I almost vomited.

Farther on, no one stopped me from looking. We walked on in a daze. Two dead Italians on the street. Then another.

The hanged man could be seen from far off. At the junction. After a telegraph pole. As we came closer, we saw that it was a hanged woman. An old woman. Xhexho broke into a dull keening.

"Kako Pino," Ilir whispered.

It was indeed her. Her skinny body swung gently in the wind. On her chest was a white rectangle with one Germanised Albanian word written on it: "saboteur."

We walked faster. Here was our alleyway. Our house. Mamma has already taken the big key from her pocket. A few more steps. But a body lies on the cobblestones with its head in a pool of blood. On the chest a piece of paper with a few words. Nazo gave a strangled cry. "Maksut!" Her daughter-in-law gazed with indifference at her husband's corpse, then stepped carefully around it, as if afraid of soiling herself with the blood. I couldn't take my eyes off the piece of paper. It read: "This is how spies will die." In that handwriting I knew so well, the letters tilted forward as if leaning into wind and rain. It was Javer's hand.

"Terrible things are going to happen. I told you so," said Xhexho, before she disappeared down the alleyway.

We all went our separate ways. Nazo and her daughter-in-law started dragging the body towards the door.

My mother had barely put the key in the lock when the door swung open by itself. Grandmother came out like a ghost.

"Come in, come in," she said in a low voice.

We went in.

"I've been waiting for you," said Grandmother.

"Maksut, out there . . . in front."

"I know. They killed him last night."

"Kako Pino . . ."

"I know," Grandmother said again. "They hanged her yesterday."

We went upstairs together.

"She was on her way to make up a bride. A patrol stopped her in the street."

"Are people still getting married in times like these?" my mother asked in surprise.

"People get married in all times," Grandmother said.

"What madness!"

"It seems it was her instruments that aroused their suspicion," Grandmother said. "They thought the metal things and the tweezers had something to do with bombs. That's what they say, at least."

I went to the window and looked out. It was cold. A searchlight threw up a frightening shaft of light, then went out.

German occupation. Greyness. Teutons. Their flag flew from the prison tower. Two s's or z's, distorted by the breeze.

Outside we could hear Nazo and her daughter-in-law, still dragging Maksut's body.

"It's going to be a merciless war," said Grandmother, putting her hand on my head.

The sound of muffled footsteps came from the street.

"People are coming back," she said. "They've been coming back in groups all night."

Again, the tender flesh of life was filling the carapace of stone.

DRAFT OF A MEMORIAL PLAQUE

A very long time later I came back to the grey immemorial city. My feet timidly trod the spine of its stone-paved streets. They bore me up. You recognised me, you stones. Often, striding along wide lighted boulevards in foreign cities, I somehow stumble in places where no one ever trips. Passersby turn in surprise, but I always know it's you. You emerge from the asphalt all of a sudden and then sink back down straight away.

My street, my cistern. My old house. Its beams, floorboards and staircase creaked slightly, almost imperceptibly, with a dry, uniform, almost constant crackling sound. What's wrong? Where does it hurt? It seemed to be complaining of aches in its bones, in its centuries-old joints.

Grandmother Selfixhe, Xhexho, Aunt Xhemo, Grandma, Kako Pino — all are gone. But at street corners, where walls join, I thought I could see some familiar features, like outlines of human faces, the shadows of cheekbones and eyebrows. They are really there, caught in stone for all time, along with the marks left by earthquakes, winters and scourges wrought by men.